THE WIDOWED BRIDE

ANNE R BAILEY

Inkblot Press

CHAPTER ONE

I had not guessed what my mama had planned for me until the day Papa told me. Sir Ralph Askew is a good match I am sure, but I have seen him only a few times and spoken to him even less. Mama is insistent that this is a great match for me. I hope you shall be there on the day as one of my bridesmaids, for you are as dear to me as my sister. Finally, I shall insist upon you visiting me at my new home in the near future...as soon as it is prudent.

—Sarah Barnette

In her fine white taffeta gown, with its delicately embroidered hem, Sarah was the quintessential bride. She took one last look in the mirror, before letting the maid adjust her bonnet on her head so it would not ruin her hair. They had spent so long pinning it up and smoothing out the frizz that it would be a shame to have the effect ruined. Sarah's hands touched the smooth lace on the bonnet. It was a beautiful piece, one that her mother had kept from her own wedding day. Overall, this was the most extravagant gown she had worn in all her life. The lace alone had cost her parents a fortune, though her mother thought it was silly she would fret over such things.

"You shall never be regarded as a fashionable lady if you become such an economical housewife," her mother said, unable to keep from chiding her.

"My husband might thank me for it," Sarah said, her eyes downcast as she played with the fringe of her scarf. This was as close as she dared come to contradicting her mother.

"What nonsense. He will appreciate you for keeping a good house and making him the envy of all his neighbours."

Sarah said nothing more but gave a little sigh. Brides should be happy on their wedding day, but she felt strangely devoid of any emotion. Perhaps it was proper. After all, in an hour or so she would cease being Sarah Barnette and become Lady Askew.

She wasn't unhappy at the prospect but simply resigned. It had been her duty to marry, and she knew that this was as good a match as she could hope for.

She was a realist. She was to inherit three thousand pounds upon the death of her father, a comfortable sum but nothing overly grand. She was comely enough, but she didn't have that flair for conversation and dance that other young ladies seemed to have. Besides this she only had her good family name; the Barnettes were well regarded and respected in the neighbourhood. It was likely owing to the relationship her father had with Sir Ralph that he even looked her way. Her father had helped pay for his schooling after his own father had lost the family fortune after a series of bad investments. Not many people knew of it, as the family had recovered a few years later. So perhaps Sir Ralph felt he owed a debt to her father. Sarah hoped he wasn't marrying her only out of charity. Maybe that explained why she felt so hesitant to say her vows.

She truly did believe her parents had chosen well. From all that she had heard about him he was a prudent man, who had been knighted for his service in the mercantile industry. His wealth had come from importing fabric from the continent. He was nearing thirty-one, a good ten years older than herself, and had very little family to speak of. Sarah only knew of a cousin on his father's side, named William Thorne, who she had met once during their courtship. He had been the only one from his side of the family to attend the ceremony and wedding breakfast.

Sarah glanced around her room. This might be one of the last times she would be in here. She tried to picture what her new home might look like. Sir Ralph had tried to describe it but was so grandiose in his descriptions that she doubted they were true.

Recently, he had purchased a small estate in Wiltshire, and he had wanted a wife to go along with it. It was because of this that Sir Ralph was in such a hurry to return to Wiltshire and urged her to set a wedding date as early as she could. However, he had promised her that on their way to their new home they would make a detour to Brighton for a bit of a honeymoon.

A glance at her mother told her she was content. She had finally stopped fretting over every little detail. Her mother's primary concern had been to see her married, and it helped that her daughter would be marrying a knight.

The clock chimed in the hallway.

Her mother hurried out of the room to see if the carriage was ready.

Just as she left, there was a little tap at Sarah's door.

"Come in," she said.

In sprang Louisa, her younger sister, only twelve years old, followed closely behind by Maria Clement, her closest friend.

"Are you ready?" Louisa said, with all the excitement of a child half her age. "You look so beautiful."

Sarah blushed, looking down at her silk slippers.

"She is right," Maria chimed in. "Here is your bouquet. I made it for you myself. And don't worry your mother has given her approval of it."

Sarah took the beautiful arrangement, examining the white roses, sage, sprigs of thyme, and lilies, all tied up with a blue ribbon.

"You must have gone to so much trouble," she said, her fingers brushing over the soft petals.

"Nonsense. Besides, it's the least I could do, seeing as you had to face the displeasure of your cousin to preserve my spot as your bridesmaid," Maria said, taking a seat across from her.

Louisa snorted; she had been witness to the curt letter that arrived, admonishing Sarah for excluding her one cousin from her bridal party. "She wouldn't even have cared if you were marrying someone without a title."

Louisa stopped chattering to examine their clothes, from her shawl to Maria's pale lilac dress. "I wish I could wear your dress instead," Louisa said, looking at Maria. "I feel so dowdy."

It wasn't the dress that made Maria look stunning but rather the contrast between it and her fair skin coupled with her dark hair. Sarah didn't bother pointing this out.

"Today is your sister's day to shine," Maria reminded her, with a wink to Sarah.

Louisa shook out her gown, a plain white dress, trying to imitate her sister's proud straight-backed stance when a thought came to her.

"Sarah, does this mean I will have to call you Lady Askew now?"

Sarah shook her head. "I would never ask you to call me that, especially not in private. You are my darling sister."

"Hmm...if I ever married a lord, or a duke, or some such person, I would like to be referred to as 'my lady' by everyone I knew."

The older two laughed.

But Louisa didn't mind, she was daydreaming as she fiddled with her own small bouquet.

At that moment her mother popped her head in the door.

"Everyone ready? Shall we head out?" She was practically squealing.

Louisa hid a laugh behind a cough, which earned her a disapproving gaze from her mother.

One last chance to arrange themselves and they were off in the carriage.

"Nervous, my dear?" her mother asked.

Sarah shook her head but squeezed Maria's hand tighter. She had a hard time admitting anything unpleasant to her mother and an even harder time doing something that would ruin her mood.

Maria was the only one she had been comfortable in sharing all her secrets and thoughts with. She was grateful she had been here.

On her mother's right sat her father in his best coat, constantly adjusting his cravat as he fixed his gaze out the window. On her mother's left was her brother, the ten-year-old Phillip who was their parents' pride and joy. This was mostly due to his being the male heir her parents had so desperately longed for.

They arrived at the church without any hiccups.

Although Sarah found herself wishing the horse would have lost a shoe and delayed their journey.

The driver opened the carriage door and her father got out first, followed by her mother, brother, Louisa, Maria, and then finally it was her turn.

She took a deep breath and promised herself that she would try to be optimistic.

She was too shy to look at Sir Ralph for long, but a quick glance his way was enough for her to gauge that he hadn't become some deformed monster overnight. He wore the typical garb a gentleman might wear on such occasions.

Someone came running up to the party. It took a moment for Sarah to recognize William Thorne. Her lips pursed at his rudeness. Had he really been about to be late for her wedding?

He tilted his hat to her mother and shook hands with her father. Sarah didn't appreciate his debonair behaviour even as her future husband clapped him on the back and asked where he had been.

"Horse threw a shoe just up the lane, but I did not wish to miss this for the world. Please accept my apologies," he said, his gaze turned to her.

She had been scowling without realizing it. Sarah forced herself to smile.

"There is nothing to forgive," she said.

"My fiancée's voice is as soothing as that of an angel. So quiet, it is like a gentle breeze on a summer day," Sir Ralph said, unable to hold back his declarations.

Sarah had to nudge Louisa who decided she couldn't contain one of her famous snorts. She herself had turned beet red. Never had someone spoken to her like this and what foolish words...

The whole company was on awkward footing, unsure how to proceed. Sarah hid behind her shyness, fixing her gaze on her bouquet.

"Shall we?" Her father took responsibility for the situation.

"Indeed, let us," Sir Ralph agreed, smiling to the left and right.

He was gone, leaving just her bridesmaid and father at the door.

"I hope you will be very happy together. He certainly seems in love with you," Maria couldn't help commenting in hushed tones as they waited for the signal to enter.

Sarah was biting the inside of her cheek. She was beginning to think her husband was a fool, but it was unfair of her to make such a judgement of him after one brief exchange.

She gave Maria a half-hearted smile.

The church organ music began playing. It was time.

"I do."

It was done so quickly and efficiently, Sarah was surprised. He placed the lightest of kisses on her cheek, and then off they went with the priest to sign the registry, with her parents and Mr. Thorne as witnesses.

The priest handed her a copy, signed and sealed.

"Hold on to that," he said.

Sarah slipped it into the pocket of her dress, later to stow it away under lock and key.

They paraded out the church handfast together.

Sarah looked ahead and to the side, anywhere but to the man whose grip was on her arm.

A few neighbours had come to wish them joy. They shouted blessings and threw flowers at them.

Her new husband helped her step into his carriage. It was new, from the cushions to the wood varnish and even the horse.

He caught her admiring and gave her an appreciative look.

"I see you can admire good quality and taste. You shall want for nothing now that we are married." He gave her a smile.

She felt a bit too much like a possession he had procured rather than a beloved wife.

They waved as the carriage set off. Her parents had left ahead of them, since they were the hosts of the breakfast and should arrive first to greet them.

They were halfway home; she was staring out the window in silence, her gloved hands on her lap, when her husband tapped the window.

"Stop the carriage," he said.

She was taken aback by this peculiar turn of events.

"We would not want to be late for the breakfast," she said with a slight stumble over her words.

"No, no. But I think now is the perfect time to get to know one's wife better," he said.

"Sir?"

"You may call me Sir Ralph. We are married now after all," he said. "We haven't talked much, but I wanted to say how much I admire you. You are everything that a wife should be, obedient, charming, and gentile. I think we shall be happy together, do you not think so?"

"Thank you for the compliment," she said, trying hard not to choke on her words.

"You shall see that I am a kind husband if you obey my wishes. I may be away from home for a long time, but I expect you to carry on looking after my home while I am gone and to uphold the best of decorum. We are to start a fabulous dynasty..."

He went on like this for quite some time. Sarah opened her mouth to say something, but he never stopped speaking for long enough for her to get out what she wanted to say.

Then to her shock he leaned forward and kissed her. Unlike earlier, this was on her mouth. He had flung himself at her so suddenly and she had been so unprepared that it ended up feeling as though he had slapped her rather than kissed her.

He pulled away, a satisfied expression on his face.

"My darling," he said as his hand grazed the side of her face.

She looked down to hide her expression of surprise and amusement but also the twinge of disgust.

"I am glad we understand each other so well," he said, sitting back with a satisfied sigh. Then he tapped on the carriage for the driver to continue.

It then occurred to Sarah that someone might have noticed the stopped carriage, that the driver might have heard what was spoken or her little gasp.

Her surprise gave way to mortification.

She had been taught to have a Christian spirit and be generous in all things, but looking across at this man, she found it hard to be charitable. She was glad to have learned that his business would take him to London a lot. She did not even care to ask what business that was.

Sarah tried to repeat to herself over and over again that she must learn to love her husband, that in time she would come to respect him. Still, it felt like something was clawing up her throat, threatening to choke her. She wanted to talk to Maria as soon as she could, but if they were to leave after the dinner, then a letter would have to suffice.

They arrived late at her home; all the guests had been assembled in the parlour and were being served buttered toast and custard tarts, but they had yet to be seated.

"Ah! There you are. We were wondering where the pair of you had got to." Her father stood up, a glass of champagne in his hand. "A toast!"

"Darling husband, we must wait." Her mother stopped him with a look of disapproval.

Sarah was glad few looked her way or made much comment about their delay. Perhaps it was normal for something like this to happen after all. She tried to force herself to smile, but she was still trying to think of a way to tolerate her new partner in life.

They were seated together side by side in the middle of the table.

Servants brought up the plates of eggs, fresh breads, and even fruit tarts. Last to be displayed to the oohs and aahs of the assembled guests was the wedding cake, a large, tiered cake, decorated with marzipan flowers and royal icing. It was a white cloud. The centrepiece of the whole affair.

Sarah would have to send off pieces to relatives who had been unable to make it to celebrate her nuptials in person. Her mother had been kind enough to supply her with a list of names.

She didn't listen to the toasts being made but politely sipped at her own glass of champagne and thanked the speaker with a smile.

Later, as people began getting up from their seats and chatting, Maria came around and placed a comforting hand on her shoulder.

"Are you well?"

Sarah tilted her head towards her to answer, when at her side her husband's sudden booming laugh made her flinch.

A few guests looked towards him in disgust

He was shoving another spoon of tart into his mouth when he said something else.

She could not hear it, but he must have found it hilarious because he began laughing, which quickly led to him pounding the table. His eyes were bulging, and he was growing red in the face but only Sarah seemed to notice.

Then, suddenly, he fell backwards followed by a loud crack as his head hit the floor. The next second was filled with horrified silence. Someone at the side of the room screamed and then they all pounced into action.

Sarah jumped to her feet, her mouth open in horror, and rushed to see what had happened. Her husband's mouth was gaping wide. She looked around her to call for help. A strange sensation of something wet sliding over her slippers made her pause. Sarah looked down again to see in horror dark red liquid pooling around him, now staining the hem of her gown.

It was then the room went black.

CHAPTER TWO

Sarah awoke to a white ceiling. She turned her head and was greeted by the familiar paisley wallpaper of her old room.

She heard someone move on the other side of the bed.

"Lady Askew, are you awake? Can you hear me?"

Sarah blinked. It took her a moment to realize that the maid was speaking to her.

"Yes," she said. She tried to sit up but her head was pounding.

"Careful, now. You'd better remain lying down. I shall fetch the doctor." The maid laid a hand on her shoulder, a gesture similar to Maria's moments before it had happened...

As her brain forced her to relive those memories she was overtaken by dizziness once again, but she fought the darkness edging her vision.

She did not have to wait long for the doctor to arrive

in his black coat, with a brown leather bag of tinctures and medicines.

"Good day, Lady Askew," he said, speaking slowly to her as though she might have trouble understanding. "I'm going to examine you, if you would allow me to."

She nodded.

He felt her pulse, listened to her heartbeat and made her drink a draft of something that burned as it went down.

"You've taken a fright, but you seem to have recovered remarkably well," he said to her before turning to the maid. "Her mother would like to know."

"Where is my mother?" Sarah suddenly thought to ask.

"She's taken to her bed. Fainted shortly after you, I am afraid, but she is recovering."

The way the doctor's lips thinned as he spoke told her that he wasn't amused by her mother's hysterics. If he wasn't getting paid for his time so well, he might have refused to call.

Sarah nodded. "Thank you for telling me. And my... husband?" Her tongue tripped over the unfamiliar word.

He coughed, shifting from one foot to another. "Perhaps I am not the one to tell you. Once your mother is sufficiently recovered—or your father, he can speak to you."

"Please, sir. I would like to know. I promise I won't faint or have a fit."

He looked doubtful but took a deep breath and a seat next to her bedside, previously occupied by her maid who was still waiting for the doctor to leave for propriety's sake.

"I am sorry to say that Sir Ralph Askew is dead. He was dead by the time I arrived, but from the sound of it he died immediately and did not suffer. The fall cracked his skull and...I am sorry for your loss," he said with all the stiffness of a man expecting an outpouring of emotion from a woman and trying to brace himself.

But Sarah defied expectations.

"Thank you for telling me. So I am a widow now?"

"I...yes." The question had stumped him.

"Oh." From bride to widow in under four hours—she was sure this must be some sort of record. It amused her slightly, but she fought to keep her features schooled. She didn't want the doctor to think she had lost her mind. Who smiled after finding out their husband had died?

"I shall let you rest in peace. Take this with a cup of tea if you feel unwell and cannot sleep." He set a bottle on her nightstand. "Lady Askew."

He was gone. The maid gave a little curtsey and told her she would go speak to her mother.

"Did you want anything before I leave?"

"No, thank you—wait, is Miss Maria still here?"

"I am afraid she was sent home, along with the other local guests," she reported and seemed truly sad to do so.

Sarah closed her eyes as it dawned on her what had just happened to her.

"I'll be going then," the maid said, and closed the door behind her.

The news would be all over town in mere hours. She

could only imagine the gossip and how her family would be shrouded by ill luck for years until hopefully talk died down.

It hadn't been her fault, but that wouldn't matter.

No wonder her mother took to her bed.

Where was her father?

She couldn't face leaving this room right now. It had always been her one sanctuary. She looked down at herself and saw that her wedding gown had been removed. She was in one of her plain day dresses, but soon she would be forced to wear black.

"What is to become of me?"

She was a widow and yet not...

Sarah had another thought and leapt to her feet, ignoring a second battering of dizziness that hit her.

The maid who had changed her had not yet removed the offending wedding dress from the room. It was wrapped and tucked away in the corner of the room, dangerously close to the fireplace.

She flinched as she touched the soft material, dreading to touch any blood that had gotten on it. At last she came to the pockets. She breathed a sigh of relief as her fingers grazed the piece of paper.

Proof of her marriage, legal proof. She clutched it to her bosom, thanking her lucky stars she still had it.

She knew vaguely she was entitled to some money if Sir Ralph Askew predeceased her. Her father had shown her the contract; he thought it would have been prudent for her to know. Perhaps it would be enough to ensure that she would not live indebted to her family for the rest of her life. Who would want a widow whose husband had died on the very day of her wedding?

If she had to live in shame at least she might have some added security and wouldn't be passed around her family like an unwanted heirloom.

She shuddered to think that a dead man was currently in her house. She had not wished to confirm whether or not this was the case. Soon the decorations in the church would be taken down and the funeral service conducted instead. Unless he was to be buried in his new parish.

She hoped she wouldn't have to make any decisions.

Sarah wanted nothing more than to be told what to do right now. But at the very least, she could ensure that she would have what was in her right to have.

She hoped never again to walk down the aisle to give herself away to another man. Especially a man like Sir Ralph Askew.

God forgive her for thinking such terrible thoughts.

She crossed herself just at the moment that her maid re-entered. A man was waiting at the threshold but had seen her. Their eyes met for a moment before he looked away, embarrassed.

"Pardon me, my lady," the maid said, "there's a gentleman who wishes to have a word with you. Mr. William Thorne."

She cleared her throat with a cough and slipped the paper into the pocket of her dress, a sense of déjà vu coming over her.

"He can come in," she said, as though he was not at her doorway and couldn't hear everything she said.

Her maid stood aside and let him come in.

He seemed uncomfortable to be in her room even though they were not alone. She couldn't help noticing how pale he was too.

He shifted from one foot to another, unsure of how to begin.

She didn't know what to say either. Nothing in her upbringing had prepared her for a moment like this.

"I suppose he shall be buried in this parish. He had not yet taken residence in his Wiltshire estate for it to be proper to have him transported and buried there. I can make all the necessary arrangements, and we will have to notify the lawyer," he said, his words coming out so fast that Sarah had to focus to make sure she caught everything he had said.

"That is very kind of you to take so much upon yourself. I agree with you; if you think it is best, then I will defer to you in this matter."

"It is a tragedy. I am sorry for your loss," he said, something akin to what one would say on such occasions to widows.

She thanked him again, then remembering that he too had lost a relation, expressed her condolence.

"I don't know how close the two of you were, but you must be very shocked and sad this terrible accident occurred. Let me know if I can help you in any way or if you need anything. I cannot speak for my family, but I am sure that you would be welcome to stay here until this matter is...dealt with." Sarah hoped she had not been overly cold or said the wrong thing. She really had not studied how to be a widow.

It felt incredibly wrong of her that the only thing she felt was resentment at the situation he had put her in. Also stress, because what would happen to her now? Widows remarried, but would anyone want a widow with such a story attached to her? People were more superstitious than they let on. Would she even want to remarry?

"Thank you for the hospitality. I am sorry to have taken up any of your time." He paused before he turned to leave, as though wanting to say something more but he wasn't sure how to phrase it.

"I shall rest, now," Sarah said, wanting him to be gone so she could be left to her own devices.

To think that if this tragic accident had not befallen her she might have been well on her way to Brighton by now.

With one last curt nod in her direction he was gone from the room.

She shared a glance with the maid who seemed to have been able to read her thoughts.

"Shall I tell them to bring your trunks back in?"

"Yes, please, and I suppose I shall have to find something more suitable to wear," Sarah said, looking down at her cream-coloured gown. She would be in black for some time to come.

"I'll see if I can dig something out," the maid said and was gone, leaving Sarah blissfully alone again.

Sarah pulled out her marriage certificate again, looking it over. This was her one escape. She did not wish to seem greedy, but it was her right by law that she should inherit whatever it was that he had left her in his will and her wedding dower. She knew she did not have proper claim to it as a wife of a few years with children would. She hoped Thorne, who was most likely his heir, would understand.

He seemed a rational sort of man, though she always seemed to be irritated by him rather than admiring or respecting him.

She peeked out her window at the courtyard; it had emptied of the carriages parked there that morning, and the garlands were also being taken down.

Everyone was rushing to hush up this wedding as if it had never taken place.

Sarah feared they would keep her hidden away.

She didn't know if she feared that more than the gossip and looks she would receive when she was next in company.

The funeral was arranged with haste and not much was asked of her. She wore one of her mother's old black dresses, altered to fit her slight frame.

She envied her younger siblings who were told to stay home. Louisa had proven unable to keep from talking about the particulars of what had occurred that day, and so she was banished to her rooms.

However, it wasn't hard to play the part of the grieving widow. With the black veil over her face it was as though she had become invisible to the world; she kept her head tilted down.

It was deemed proper of her not to be wailing and making a scene, but many of the people who had attended the wedding also attended the funeral out of curiosity to see the woman who had been widowed on the very day of her wedding.

It was then anger rose within her. Surely she couldn't be the only one who this had happened to? What about her second cousin whose fiancé had died before the wedding? There had been hot tears shed then, but two years later she had remarried and now had two children to show for it.

After the funeral, Maria came to visit her, using the excuse of wanting to comfort her friend.

They were served tea in the drawing room; only Louisa was with them on this day.

"How is your mother?" Maria asked, noticing her absence.

Sarah gave her a tight-lipped smile. "She's been keeping to her room most days and cannot stand to see me otherwise she tends to burst into tears. I've taken to having my meals brought to my room so she can emerge safely from her rooms."

"You are too kind." Maria's expression spoke volumes about what she thought about this.

But despite everything Sarah couldn't bring herself to

criticize her mother. It was against every principle she had ever been taught.

"I am trying to make it easier on everyone," she began saying but was interrupted by a loud sigh coming from Louisa.

Her sister had set her book down and thrown herself down on the couch.

"Louisa, that is very unladylike," Sarah couldn't help but admonish her.

"What does it matter? Nothing matters anymore. Mother says we cannot go to parties and no one comes to visit. No offence, Maria. It has been so dull," Louisa complained. The bitterness was evident in her every word.

"I know it must be hard for you," Maria said as sympathetically as she could but shared a private smile with Sarah at the dramatics displayed by her.

"We are waiting for the lawyer to come up from London and then matters should settle down more. Our guest"—by that she had been referring to Mr. Thorne— "shall likely leave after that."

"What of you?" Maria pressed on. "What shall become of you?"

"Nothing for now. I am to be in mourning at least for the year; it is only proper."

"But you barely knew him," Louisa piped up.

"We were married under the sight of God. People wouldn't care if we hated each other; we still have to observe the correct protocol on such occasions," Sarah said. Though it was getting harder to remember it herself.

"You shall learn, Louisa," Maria joined in.

Louisa rewarded her by sticking out her tongue.

The other two women laughed even though they knew it should have been their duty to reprimand her behaviour. In a few years it would no longer be acceptable for Louisa to be running around behaving so rashly like a wild child.

"And what about you?" Sarah asked Maria. "Are you attending the assembly ball? We heard about it from my aunt."

Maria nodded. "But I shall miss seeing you there. I suppose it would hardly be appropriate for you to come out in society."

Sarah chuckled. "We didn't even receive an invitation, so I think whether or not I wanted to go does not matter. Tell me, have you heard any talk about me? What do they say?"

Maria, usually an outspoken young lady, was looking down at her lap.

"You can tell me. I'd rather be prepared than walk around not knowing what people were saying behind my back."

A sigh escaped Maria's lips. "The word around town is that at the sight of you he fainted and died. That's the meanest of the rumours. The others are a variation of the truth. The actual truth sounds equally ridiculous."

Sarah felt a pang of hurt at the insinuation of that first, meanest rumour, but it could have been worse.

"Good, I hope it shall all blow over. I am not sure I can get used to wearing my widow's garb though."

"On the other hand, you've now become an eligible chaperone. Everyone will have to have you."

Sarah laughed. "They will be disappointed. I would not be any less strict than an old matron or their mothers. I really don't understand this chasing around for eligible bachelors as some ladies seem keen on doing. Maybe I can be an example to them. Would you like more tea?" She had noticed her friend's cup now contained nothing more than dregs.

"No, I am quite satisfied. I am also glad that you seem to have recovered so well."

They continued talking for most of the afternoon, entertaining themselves with what-ifs, until at last the sun began dipping low.

"I had better take my leave of you. I shall try calling on you soon. My mother seems keen on finding me a match. I suppose even your fiasco hasn't dampened her enthusiasm."

"You are her last daughter at home. Of course she wants to see you settled. But I would rather you stayed around here longer. I would hate to lose you so quickly."

"Perhaps you can point me in the direction of a man who seems likely to die on my wedding day as well. Then we could live out our remaining days as happy widows together."

This set all three of them to laughing.

"If only it was so easy. Though I would not wish such ill luck on anyone. Hopefully, mother will think it is acceptable for me to go for a walk soon. I never thought I would miss fresh air as much as I do now."

Sarah sighed. "Farewell. Take my well wishes to all your family."

Maria nodded, and gave Louisa a pat on the head.

"Take care of your sister."

Louisa grinned and said she would. "I will sneak her off to the garden dressed as a maid. What fun!"

Sarah rolled her eyes. That was all she needed. She could only imagine the talk that would spring forth then.

It was a dreary few days as she waited anxiously for the lawyer to arrive.

William Thorne had kept to his rooms, but from her vantage point in the parlour Sarah could see that he occasionally rode out.

After nearly a whole week of seclusion her mother emerged from her sick bed and could stand to be in the same room with her. However, she couldn't seem to stop frowning whenever she looked her way.

"Mother, please stop. I did nothing wrong, and of course I wish none of this had ever happened," Sarah tried pleading with her but to no avail. All that would inspire was her mother beginning a new lecture on how she had managed to bring misfortune upon the whole family.

"You know if you weren't the oldest then at least there would have been a chance that your other siblings could have made respectable matches without the stain of this incident following after them."

Sarah opened her mouth to reply but was forced to keep quiet as her mother continued.

"Now, I can hardly imagine what sort of family would wish to engage themselves to your younger siblings. We shall never outlive this scandal."

"Mother, it is hardly a scandal. It is a tragedy. Think of the Hardwells, whose daughter eloped to Gretna Green. They faced a year of censure, but now all is well. Louisa has at least six years before she would even consider marriage; by then all of this would have blown over."

Her rational arguments seemed to fall on deaf ears.

Often her only respite was when William Thorne joined them for supper. Then her mother was silent, as her disdain for her turned towards William, the heir apparent.

"When shall the lawyer arrive from London? I suppose he's been delayed on the roads," she said quite rudely one night.

Even Sarah's father choked on his food, coughing a bit in surprise.

"He wrote to me that he was departing about two days ago. He should arrive any day now."

"I suppose he does not keep his own carriage and must make do with hired coaches." Her mother frowned, looking quite put out.

"We must be grateful he would be willing to undertake such a journey," Sarah said, though her quiet words went unheard except by William Thorne, who for once spared her a tiny smile.

They had never been on friendly terms.

When they had been introduced he had looked at her as though she was some great husband-hunter taking advantage of the goodwill of his cousin and had forced him into marriage.

She didn't know what Sir Ralph had told him, but he had seemed to be irked by her before she had even said two words to him. They had spent the whole evening in each other's company, but he had been set upon avoiding her as much as possible. He did not even speak to her when by chance they were partnered to play cards.

She thought that he had overcome his dislike of her, but lately it had seemed to grow into a deep annoyance. It usually showed on his face whenever she caught him looking her way. Perhaps he found her ridiculous in her mother's altered gowns.

She had ordered new material and a gown to be made for her. One for day wear and evening. If her mother were to insist on her wearing full mourning then the expense would have to be made. This altered dress was fine for the morning, but she couldn't go out in it.

"Mother, may I go on a walk with Maria tomorrow?" Sarah asked. "Just through the gardens and down to the stream?" She hoped the change in conversation would make her mother remember to be civil.

"You are in mourning. The deepest of mourning. What would happen if people saw you traipsing around the countryside?"

"Mother—"

"I always found walks lovely to refresh the spirits,"

William said, dabbing the corner of his mouth with his napkin. "Miss Sarah seems paler than usual."

"Miss Sarah?" Her mother rounded on him. "She is Lady Askew."

"I am sorry, I forgot. The marriage was so brief." William flashed a toothy grin.

Sarah was mortified that he was going head-to-head with her mother.

"Darling, before you go spoiling your appetite, I don't think there's anything wrong with Sarah going for a walk around the grounds. It is not as though she is dancing at a ball." Her father seemed to have awoken from his stupor.

She was so grateful for his intervention.

"Very well," her mother said, giving way to him as she always did, especially around company.

"Well, that is settled then. What is all this ridiculous argument about walks? These last few weeks I have quite been put out. I am done with it. I want to hear no more talk of widows and propriety." Her father set down his fork rather forcibly, making her flinch, a motion not missed by Thorne.

Sarah hoped Maria would be pleased by the note she was sending her, that she would be somewhat released.

"Please come by anytime you wish tomorrow, I should love your company—Your Friend, Sarah"

Her brother Phillip had been largely keeping away from her too. She had found this peculiar but didn't have time to dwell on it. He was still holed up with a school master most days, learning mathematics and Latin. Her father had hopes that one day he would become a judge or take up some professional calling. It was well regarded when a gentleman had a good education under his belt.

As Sarah was tying her bonnet, her maid brought her a dark brown parasol. She looked at it curiously. It was a sunny day, but it hardly called for a bonnet and parasol.

"Your mother sends this to you," she said.

"Is she hoping that people won't notice me going out for a stroll? This would only draw more attention to me." Sarah looked at it in wonder.

Just then William Thorne appeared, and she took the parasol without another word of complaint. She didn't want him to hear her complaining.

He caught sight of her and tipped his hat in greeting towards her.

"Good day, Lady Askew," he said.

"Good day, Mr. Thorne," she replied with equally cool civility. But then she checked herself, remembering it was to him that she was indebted for her freedom. "I wanted to thank you, sir, for intervening last night. You did not have to trouble yourself, but I am grateful you did."

He paused mid-step and gave her a nod. "To be honest with you, Lady Askew, I think I did it more for the sake of arguing with your mother than helping you, but I am glad something good came out of it."

Sarah looked down at her feet, fighting to keep her

embarrassment down. Of course he had not willingly been acting as her champion.

"She can be a handful at times. Her emotions get the better of her, but you didn't hear it from me." She gave him a half-hearted little smile.

Which he returned with a mere nod.

"I'll leave you to your walk then," he said and left as fast as he could without running off.

Was she truly so terrifying he couldn't stand her presence?

"Maria is here!" Louisa came bounding in through the open door. "She's waiting in the lane."

"Then I shall head out. Are you joining us, Louisa?" Sarah thought it would be polite to ask even though she was hoping to speak to Maria alone.

"No, I want to try fishing in the pond. Phillip said he caught a fish that was bigger than Pike."

"Well, did you see this large fish?"

"No, he said Pike stole him, and gobbled him up before he could show me."

"Hmm." Sarah was sceptical about the story. It was true the spaniel had a love of fish they all found amusing. He had earned his name when he had sneaked into the kitchen one day and stolen a pike off the chef's table, ignoring the large ham sitting there.

She still remembered when their mother had bought the tiny spaniel. They were at the height of fashion one season, but this dog had proved unwilling to be a lapdog. From the earliest days he had preferred the company of the children and ran after them on their romps. He had the energy of a hunting dog despite being the size of a large rabbit.

"Well, make sure Pike doesn't get hold of your fish," Sarah suggested.

"Oh, I won't. I am keeping him far away from me today."

Sarah smiled indulgently at her and then left.

A cool breeze hit her as she stepped outside for the first time since the funeral. It felt wonderful to feel the sun on her face again.

Maria waved at her from the lane, and she responded in kind but urged her to come towards her.

"I am afraid that my mother says I must keep to our land, but we can walk through the gardens or even up to the small wood."

"She's really trying to hide you away, isn't she?" Maria looked at her, full of pity. "Well, slowly but surely you shall escape her efforts."

"Shall I indeed?" Sarah said with a chuckle. "When have I ever been able to escape her without help?"

"Well, you are here now."

"Only because a certain someone took my part at supper last night," she said, confessing the truth.

"Oh? Is this the same someone who is staying with your family?"

"Yes, it is. William Thorne has both infuriating and a great help. I cannot wait until I no longer have to share a roof with him. To be fair to him he does keep to himself most of the time. I do wish I knew why he seems to dislike me so much..." While taking in the sights, she thought to herself of the possible reasons for this.

"Too bad he is so disagreeable, otherwise I might set my cap at him," Maria said with a teasing tone.

"Maria! You cannot possibly mean that." Sarah frowned, imagining her friend walking down the aisle with Mr. Thorne.

"He is quite good looking, and if it is true that he is Sir Ralph's heir then he is also a good catch," Maria said in all seriousness.

"If you are truly interested, then you may pursue him. Don't stop an acquaintance on my behalf," Sarah said.

Maria waved her off. "He wouldn't look at me. He's proven to be too prudent a man to fall for my charms."

"And they are very great charms indeed," Sarah complimented her, mimicking her teasing tone of voice.

This earned her a laugh. "If I had more than a thousand a year, I am sure I would have a line of suitors out the door, but such as it is I am happy. I am not in a rush to get married, and I have plenty of siblings who would be happy to have a nursemaid for their many children."

"I wouldn't wish that life for you. I've had to play that part to my siblings, and they can be quite exhausting. It would be much easier to have a house of your own and delegate tasks to nurses and maids."

"Maybe, if my father takes us to London this autumn, I'll be able to catch myself a wealthy old baron. Then I would have nothing to do but sit around eating bonbons and cakes..."

"Don't forget entertaining your dearest friends," Sarah said, lest she be forgotten in her friend's schemes.

"That goes without saying. Of course you shall be my constant companion. We shall travel the continent on his fortune."

"He might not enjoy that, and you know how I hate travelling."

Maria looked disappointed. "You are no fun. Travelling isn't so bad. I see it as a grand adventure."

"When have you ever been on a boat? I went once on a river cruise and was sick the whole time. I could not imagine going on the oceans for weeks on end."

"Then I shall leave you at home to tend my old husband and I shall find a paramour to take with me."

Sarah gasped, shocked at such a statement coming out of her mouth.

"What? You are a married woman—you should know about such things by now," Maria said, nudging her gently.

"I do not," Sarah said, her voice barely audible.

Maria's grin widened. "You mean you weren't exchanging love letters and other tokens of affection with that man?"

Sarah shook her head.

"A pity, but at least you are not heartbroken over his loss." She stopped walking and opened up her purse, pulling out a small book and handing it to Sarah.

"I am letting you borrow this since I think you might need it more than me."

Sarah looked at the cover. *Hymns for Ladies*, read the

title. Her eyebrow rose at her friend, who was not only one of the least religious people she knew but also not a great reader.

"Look inside," Maria prompted her, seeing her amusement.

Sarah opened the book and saw that instead of devotional hymns there was actually something quite different. The title card on the first page read: *Roxana*.

"What is this?"

"Read it and you shall find out. It's quite shocking," Maria said with a wistful smile. "Some might call it romantic."

Sarah nearly dropped it but tucked it away in the pocket of her gown.

"Wherever did you get such a thing?"

"My sister Isabelle's library. Last summer I grew quite bored and found this among her collection. I bet she is missing it, but she can hardly dare accuse me of anything without revealing herself. I see your disapproval, my friend. I shall return it to her in due time," Maria said and, with that, took her arm and led her away back up the lane towards the row of trees in the distance.

"This is why my mother says widows should stay inside. If she ever found out, she would have my head."

"Say it was a gift from your dearly departed husband. Maybe she will think less of him if he gifted you things like *Roxana*," Maria snorted. "But I do hope things shall be settled for you, and rather soon too. I hate to see you in such distress."

"It is only dealing with my family, and I am worried

about what people are saying or thinking. Some mornings I wake up and I quite forget where I am and what has happened. Those moments are so blissful."

Maria tried to console her with a pat on her arm.

"Shall I stay for tea or head home?"

"You had better head home. I don't mean to be rude, but if my mother is in a foul temper it would be best you weren't around to witness it," Sarah said, playing with the gloves she wore.

"I cannot wait for you to change out of this dowdy dress as well. Surely you cannot be forced to wear such a sad colour for a whole year," Maria said. "If the marriage were to be annulled—"

"No," Sarah was quick to say. "No, it could not be."

"Why ever not?"

Now Sarah flushed. "We were late to the breakfast because he stopped the carriage on the way home..."

"No!" Maria was truly shocked.

Sarah looked around to make sure no one could overhear. "He...well, first he talked a lot and then he leapt at me."

"Oh, I am so sorry. How awful for you. I had no idea..."

Sarah brushed away her worries. "But, you see, I could never swear truthfully that I did not know my husband in that way...besides, I would not wish to lose what I was entitled to. No one else will have me, and I would hate to be a burden on my family. If somehow this would help then I cannot throw away a chance for financial independence."

Maria looked at her appreciatively. "You always had a mind for numbers. Very rational of you to think that way. Perhaps too rational."

"Ha," Sarah said. "I am not a fool."

Sarah couldn't find a moment by herself to read *Roxana* without the risk of discovery. No one in her house seemed to respect the privacy of her room, even since her widowhood.

So, as she retired to bed, she sneaked an extra candlestick upstairs with her.

Snuggled up in a heavy robe, she sat at her desk and tried her best to read the words by the dim light. As though she could hear her mother in her head, she thought about how this would ruin her eyes, but bravely she ignored her worries and cracked open the well-worn pages of the book.

It did not take her long to be blushing from head to toe at the words written inside, as a tale of lust and unrequited desire unfolded itself to her. And yet she didn't put it down; it was too entertaining. Too shocking.

The candles had nearly burned out before she had finished. It must be very late into the night, but she dared not check the clock outside her room.

Laying her head down on her pillow, her dreams were filled with sordid recreations of what she had read.

CHAPTER THREE

"Y ou cannot be serious, sir." William Thorne was fuming.

Sarah thought she could spy steam escaping from his head.

She had forbidden her mother and father from being here for the reading of her husband's will. Though, she had agreed to her maid being in the room as a chaperone and witness. She was glad she had told them they might speak to the lawyer after. Her mother would have been unable to keep silent at Thorne's outbursts.

"I am very serious, sir," the lawyer said, adjusting the spectacles on his nose. "It was stated very clearly in the marriage contract, and the late Sir Ralph Askew also wrote to me himself to amend his will. I am afraid his wishes were made very clear."

Sarah flinched as Thorne's gaze turned to her. The burning anger there made her wish she would sink into the cushions of the seat.

They were in her father's office, with its oak panelling and dim lighting. This ambience, added to William Thorne's expression, made him seem absolutely frightening.

"I did not write the will nor the marriage contract," she said to him once she found her voice. "There's no need to look at me as though I have stolen the rug from under you."

His lips thinned.

"Perhaps not, madam. But I can see your father and mother's meddling in this. My cousin was indebted to your father; he might have felt coerced into agreeing to this." He made a sweeping gesture with his hand over the papers laid before them.

"If he was indebted or felt like he was, then there could be no coercion. My father did not have the means to force him to act against his wishes. He freely paid for Sir Ralph's schooling and living expenses at the time. There was no formal contract. So what Sir Ralph agreed to afterwards was not at my father's insistence. It could not have been. Especially if it was distasteful to Sir Ralph. I am sure he meant for us to...have children and wanted to ensure they were looked after in case of his untimely demise." She surprised herself with how coherently she expressed herself in such a tense moment.

Her words checked William Thorne, but his eyes seemed to narrow further.

She had the impulse to tell him that if he continued frowning like that he might find his expression stuck like that forever. She would try to sketch out his face to show

Maria at some later date. Perhaps she would change her opinion of him as a handsome man.

"Sir, I suggest we adjourn and collect ourselves. This is a very stressful time," the lawyer said, looking at the clock on the mantle.

"An excellent suggestion." Sarah turned her challenging gaze on William, who, seeing he was outnumbered, could only agree.

"Perfect." The lawyer clapped his hands together. "And, Lady Askew, if I could please have some refreshments brought to me here, I will continue my work in the office."

Sarah nodded and turned her head to her maid to send the instructions to the kitchen.

"We shall reconvene in thirty minutes then," the lawyer said, dismissing them as though they were a pair of errant schoolchildren.

She stood and walked out of the room, but she hadn't gotten far before a grip on her elbow stopped her in her tracks.

Sarah looked at the offending hand in surprise before looking up to see who it was. She was not shocked to see that William Thorne was the perpetrator.

She pulled her arm away. He looked apologetic, but the words died on his lips.

He cleared his throat before continuing.

"This is a sham. You cannot lay claim to one third of his estate," he said, trying his best to seem civil.

Sarah knew him better by now. If he thought she was some fortune hunter, then he was no better.

"I have nothing to say to you that I did not say in the room. If it is my right as his widow, then I shall claim it. Once I die, you shall have it back in your keeping," she said.

His face had gone dark, and Sarah wondered if he was contemplating hastening that event.

"This is my only security. You must see that, but perhaps you do not. But who would want to marry me now? I have an infamous reputation." She saw the surprise on his face. "What? Did you think I did not see what was printed in the gossip column about me?" she said, tears stinging her eyes, but she tried to get a hold of herself. "It is my right as his widow, even if our marriage lasted such a short time. That is the law."

He was smirking now, a cynical amused expression, as he leaned forward towards her.

Sarah could feel his breath on her face as she fought the urge to step away from him.

"I doubt you were his wife in every sense of the word. So there is no need to keep up the pretence of being his heartbroken widow. I know you rarely spoke and hardly seemed to tolerate his presence. I could have the marriage annulled and then you would be owed nothing," he said, threat dripping from every word.

"And I would contradict you. It was indeed a true marriage." She could feel her cheeks beginning to burn in anger and embarrassment as she replied. "What would you require from me to prove it?"

Even as she said the words, she regretted them. But

there was no taking them back. She would later blame *Roxana* as she retold the tale to Maria.

For the first time that day, William Thorne seemed at a loss. He was the one to step away, his eyebrows rising in shock.

Had she overstepped the mark? Not any more than he had. But tempers were high on both sides.

"Is that all, sir?" she spat out.

"Yes," he coughed, spinning on his heel and leaving her alone in the hallway.

Sarah released a breath and ran to her room, shutting the door behind her. She dabbed the corner of her eyes with a handkerchief and splashed cool water on her face.

When it was time to return to the lawyer's office, she hoped she no longer looked as red as a beet.

William was already seated, and she took the seat to the left of his.

They waited as a servant cleared away the tea tray that had been brought up to the lawyer.

"Well, I have looked over everything and it seems to be in order. You have a few options before you, Mr. Thorne. First, if it suits you better, you can buy out Lady Askew's half, or second, the two of you could come to some sort of agreement between the pair of you. As it stands legally, she is entitled to a third of the revenue of the estate, which comes to about one thousand pounds if the paperwork is correct. I know this is all highly unusual, but it is what it is. You may try to contest it in court, but I doubt you would be very successful, seeing as both the marriage contract he signed and the will he amended are in accordance," he said.

William Thorne seemed defeated but was trying to rally his spirits. He thanked the attorney and returned to his rooms.

"I shall leave by tomorrow morning," he said to her as he walked through the doorway.

Sarah stared after him for a moment before turning her attention to the attorney.

"Thank you, sir. Please let me know if there is anything else I can be of help with. Are you staying for supper?" she said with a calm air of politeness.

"Thank you, I shall inquire with your butler about the times of the coach. I shall have to head back home as soon as I can. Plenty of business for me to look into and all that."

She nodded, sympathetic to his plight. "I shall speak to someone directly. My father would likely wish to have a word with you as well before you leave, if you will humour him."

"Of course."

She stood and bade him farewell.

Her heart was light as she walked up the stairs to the upper floor and hid in her room. She had gained more than she thought she possibly could. She could envision herself renting out a small cottage somewhere and living out the rest of her days comfortably.

It was a good dream to have.

But she could foresee how Thorne would be a thorn in her side.

She was also unsure of what she would do next. Should she travel to Wiltshire? What would be required of her? There was so much her family had never prepared her for. So much she would have to teach herself.

By the end of the week the house had emptied of all visitors, wanted and unwanted.

But peace was far from restored in the house.

Sarah was constantly pressured by her mother to sign over her financial assets to her father.

"There is no need for you to worry about such matters," her mother said, driving a needle painfully fast through her embroidery.

"Let your father take care of everything for you. What do you know about investing? You have everything you could possibly need."

"But, Mother, it is my money. You have your own pocket money that you spend as you please. I don't want to go begging to Father for every shilling to buy a piece of ribbon."

Her mother waved her off. "You have your allowance. How will this be any different? Think of it, we can make some improvements to the house and send your brother off to the best schools. The extra income would go a long way."

Sarah frowned. "But it is my money. It is the money

of the Askew estate. I am entitled to it, but I should not spend it enriching our family. It would not seem right."

"Selfish girl. After all your father and I have sacrificed for you."

Luckily before this back-and-forth exchange could continue, Louisa and Pike came running in, distracting her mother.

"Louisa, your dress is so dirty. What happened?"

Sarah could see the mud splatter going up the dress.

Louisa was unabashed though. "I was playing with Pike, and I accidentally ran through a muddy puddle. I am sorry about the mess I made."

Her mother seemed unconvinced that she was truly sorry.

Sarah left the drawing room with the excuse she wanted to go sketch outside. She had been grateful that her new gown had arrived. This simple black dress suited her more, and by the grace of it being fitted to her properly, also looked nicer. Throwing on a brown apron, she took her stencils and sketchbook to find a suitable spot to sketch from.

She worked on a landscape of the house, having a hard time getting the shrubbery down.

It was unsurprising, as her mind was so distracted by the conversation she had been having with her mother. This was her moment of true freedom. Her parents had no rights to her dower revenue, and she wasn't about to hand it over. Sarah loved and respected her parents, but this was too much.

"There you are."

A voice behind her shook her out of her reverie. She looked up to see her father; his face seemed aged and tired.

"May I join you?"

She nodded, and he sat beside her, examining her sketch.

"You manage to capture the house so beautifully," he said, stretching out his legs. "I wanted to talk to you. Your mother has been unable to hold her tongue, or so she tells me."

Sarah set down her pencil, readying herself for a lecture, but none came.

"Life is always unexpected, but you must decide what to do with the cards you have been dealt. Neither your mother nor I have a legal say over what you do with yourself or even your money. That is just simply the fact. But you do realize, or are coming to realize, that you cannot stay here anymore."

"What do you mean?" Sarah said; her heart was beating faster as her anxiety mounted. Was he throwing her out of her home?

He smiled at her, a kind smile that she hadn't seen much of.

"You are a widow now. Your name has been dragged through the mud in the newspapers, but you have been granted your independence financially. Your mother is who she is and will never let you have your peace."

"So what am I to do?" she said, tears springing to her eyes.

He looked sympathetic. "You were to leave us a few

weeks ago and begin your life away from the family. You must consider that you will have to do that again. Your mother will hound you if you remain here. This is your chance to take your destiny into your own hands."

She shook her head. "You've always told me what to do. Why are you saying this to me now?"

"I've always done what was required of me as your father. I raised you, saw to your welfare and that you had everything you desired. I arranged a marriage I thought would provide you with security and a comfortable home. Now that has been altered, but we cannot predict the future. You must make your own way—if you want peace. We would never turn you away, but you can imagine how things will be if you remain here," he said, taking her trembling hands in his.

"You cannot be afraid. Think that many young ladies do not have the luxury of this choice. You must consider it. I will not push you one way or another."

She had begun crying and had not even realized it until the tears dripped down her face and onto her lap. The prospect of leaving was so terrifying. It was more terrifying than when she had been told that her marriage was arranged. At that time it had been others making decisions for her.

Now she was facing the future with only herself as a guide. She could set sail for the Americas if she wanted to. No one was constraining her actions anymore. It was both exhilarating and frightening to realize.

"Hush now," he said, handing her a handkerchief from his pocket.

Grateful, she took it and wiped her eyes.

"You do not need to make a decision at this very moment. But it had occurred to me that no one has told you that you could make this decision."

"Thank you, Father."

He patted her shoulder. "I'll see you at supper."

She watched him make his way back home. Her heart swelled with affection for him. He had never been the most involved father, preferring to leave matters to her mother, but he had a sense of righteousness that she appreciated now more than ever.

Desperately she wanted to speak to Maria about this. The only other soul she felt she could confide in. But she knew deep down that this was a decision she had to make on her own. Her father was right. She was free. No one might wish to marry her now, but it did not matter. If she lived a modest lifestyle, she was free until she died.

How would William Thorne react?

She knew that she had the right to remain on the estate, and for now that would have to suffice. According to the will she should be entitled to live in a small cottage on the estate or even have a set of rooms assigned to her. For now she just needed a refuge until she came up with a plan.

She picked up a pen and pulled a fresh sheet of paper towards her.

Louisa had been clinging to her all morning.

"You absolutely cannot go," she said.

To her credit she did not cry. Yet, Sarah's guilt was rising ever higher.

"It does not mean we shall never see each other again," she said. "Besides, once I am settled you could come and visit me, and I shall take you all around my new house and spoil you rotten."

Louisa grumbled something under her breath.

Out of the corner of her eye Sarah could see the smile cross her mother's lips. They were not on speaking terms, not even for lectures now. She had not realized how much of the conversation she had with people all day revolved around her mother's lectures.

If her mother was amused by her plight, she would not allow her to see how much she was wavering in her decision.

Phillip had seemed the most unaffected by all of the developments. He had long ago resigned himself to the fact that his older sister and one-time nursemaid was leaving the house. To him this was a natural progression of events.

"Are you no longer cursed now?" he had asked her one evening as the family was sitting down around the fire after dinner.

Sarah had nearly choked on her tea.

"I don't believe I was ever cursed. God forbid," she said, feeling the need to cross herself. "If anything, you could say I came about some good fortune lately."

He had nodded, as solemn as their father.

After that encounter he had no longer avoided her

company or worried that somehow her curse would rub off on him. Sarah wasn't sure where he had gotten such foolish ideas, but her mother had shown her one of the first newspapers that had printed a story about her.

She had been furious and wondered if there was some way she could get them to stop.

Maria had assured her that in time it would blow over. There was nothing new to write about, and they would find some other topic to get their newspapers selling again.

Ever the fount of wisdom, Maria had been proven correct.

A month after the unhappy incident, there was no more mention of her. She knew it would take longer for it to be forgotten about by people, but at least her mother had stopped receiving cut-outs of every article their kind relatives had found.

The news had travelled as far as Wales, as far as she could tell. She supposed she should be impressed or proud to have become such an overnight sensation.

Her dearest friend was a frequent visitor the last weeks of her stay before her move.

"I am very excited for you. Are you sure you would not hire me on to be your companion?" she had asked, a twinkle of amusement in her eyes.

"Your mother would have my head. But I would love it if you could accompany me there. I shall be terribly scared to be alone."

"I shall ask my mother," Maria said. "Though, to be

truthful, she's been against my associating with you so much."

"Oh." Sarah looked away from her, downcast.

Only a light touch on her arm made her look up again.

"You can be sure that I told her I did not care a fig about what she thought. You are my best friend, and I would not forsake you now. Plus, you are a wealthy widow," she said with a wink.

Sarah chuckled. "You did not!"

Maria rolled her eyes. "I guess you know me well enough by now. But I did say something along those lines. And don't worry, I am being incredibly selfish. If I took a trip with you, I would be escaping my mother's plots to marry me off to anyone with over four thousand a year, regardless of age, appearance, or temper. On top of it all, I would get to see the dashing Thorne again," she said, clutching her hands to her chest in a dramatic fashion.

They were coming up to a hedge that, upon further inspection, was an overgrown rose bush.

"You are joking, and I shall pretend I did not hear you," Sarah said, examining the pretty flowers. They were small but the colours so vibrant it was a shame that this part of the grove wasn't tended more regularly.

"You claim that you are great enemies, but you are practically moving in with him," Maria said, as she carefully plucked a rose, bringing it to her nose to smell. "You move quite quickly, my dear friend."

Sarah was flabbergasted.

"Y-you know that...I hate him."

"Do you really?" The arched eyebrow stopped Sarah, who prayed for patience with her mischievous friend.

"I strongly dislike him. Solely for the reason that he seems to despise me, even though I have done absolutely nothing to him. He's also trying to stop me from claiming my rights. I understand why he might not be pleased about losing a third of his land but...I never took him for a greedy man."

Maria considered her for a moment. "It is a mystery you shall have to uncover. Rest assured, if you are poisoned I shall notify the authorities about who their chief suspect should be."

Sarah gasped. "Now, you cannot be serious that he would do that. I cannot imagine anyone stooping to such levels."

Maria looked at her as though she was a fool.

"Maria, this isn't one of your silly little books," Sarah said, then suddenly remembered and pulled the disguised *Roxana* from her pocket. "Here you go."

Maria thanked her, slipping it back into her dress.

"Did you like it?"

Sarah blushed. "I did. It was quite shocking at first, and I am not surprised you would bring up poisoning after reading it."

"At least I did not bring up abduction," Maria said, laughing.

They left the rose bush alone and walked on, heading back towards the house.

"Do such things really happen?" Sarah said, unable to keep her thoughts to herself.

Maria shrugged. "Not that I have heard, but I could see it. Especially if one was a beautiful rich heiress. Maybe you will have chances now."

"Luckily I have a curse hanging over me," Sarah pointed out.

"You should see someone about that," Maria said with one last laugh.

They reached the house and Sarah invited Maria inside for a cup of tea, but she declined. "If you truthfully want me to accompany you to Wiltshire, I shall go and speak to my mother this very moment."

"I'll call on you tomorrow to find out the news," Sarah said, in a buoyant mood. "I hope you shall be able too. A friendly face in a strange place will be a boon."

She was looking over an inventory of items for her departure, checking over the packed luggage. Her father had generously donated the family carriage for her and arranged a trusted footman to accompany herself, Maria, and a maid.

It had irritated her mother, and she suspected that this was the revenge her father extracted for the weeks of misery he had been forced to endure. Her mother's displeasure with her had caused her to lash out at everyone in her vicinity.

They departed on a warm August morning.

Ready for a new start, Sarah tried her best to keep her worries at bay. This wouldn't be goodbye forever, so she shouldn't be melodramatic about it. At least she would try not to be. Besides, hadn't she been preparing to say goodbye to her home and family since her engagement? She looked out the windows at the familiar landscape, trying to commit the view to memory, fearing her crude sketches would not be enough.

CHAPTER FOUR

The picturesque landscape of Wiltshire was enough to offset some of Sarah's homesickness. The journey had been long, and she had not allowed much time for rest; she had wanted to reach her new home as soon as possible and establish herself before Thorne could change his mind.

Her companions were all sleeping as the carriage came lumbering up the lane into the small village of Bluehaven.

It was a pretty little place with only a shop or two and an inn. It seemed like just the peaceful sort of tranquillity she would enjoy.

Maria awoke with a start after the carriage wheel passed over a particularly large bump in the road.

"I will never get used to sleeping in carriages," Maria said with a yawn while rubbing the side of her head.

"I admire you for being able to even catch a moment

of rest," Sarah said. She had been unable to sleep much at all, even at night tucked away in the bed of an inn.

The driver stopped at the inn to ask the owner for directions.

Sarah did not get out of the carriage, eager not to cause any delays.

"It's not far, your ladyship," the innkeeper said, coming out to greet them. Clearly nosy about the newcomers rather than trying to be helpful. "Down the main road here and within a mile you will come to a fork in the road. Take a left and not long after you will find Oakham."

"Thank you for your assistance," she said, keeping back from thanking him with more exuberance as she caught him staring at her dress. Perhaps he had not heard of her coming or wasn't expecting to see a widow come travelling down the lane.

They drove on and indeed within the next half hour they had arrived. Large stone pillars indicated the entrance to the estate. The plaque fitted there looked new and ostentatious in its presentation. She wondered who had commissioned it, her late husband or his heir?

Maria couldn't help but point it out too, an amused grin spreading across her face, though she didn't comment further.

The drive was small, considering how large the entrance was, and was little more than a well-beaten track. As they approached the main part of the estate, it seemed as though work had begun on the foundation of a proper road. Upon further inspection it was clear that a lot of work had been started on the house here and there, but every project—from the removal of the ivy clinging to the house to the pruning of overgrown shrubbery—was left unfinished.

A moment of dread filled her as she regarded this dismal scene. This would have been her marital home? It was hardly the grand estate her husband had described. He had said he had gotten a good bargain, but that was no wonder seeing the state of it.

The carriage came to a stop at the entrance, and a man came out to greet them with a bow.

"Lady Askew, I presume?" He spoke to Maria, as the driver helped her out of the carriage first.

"I am afraid not," she said, and moved aside for Sarah to emerge.

He bowed. "Apologies. It is a pleasure to meet you. The master was expecting you. He's in the drawing room."

"And our things?" Sarah said, looking to the trunks piled high on the carriage.

"They shall be looked after. Your rooms have been prepared for you," the butler said, with a bow of his head. He led them inside.

The entrance was grand and open. There was something off again in the choice of decor. Too many accents of gold here and there seemed to clash with the house. It seemed like it belonged in a different sort of residence but was being made to fit here. This building was not nearly grand enough to house gold knobs and sconces.

"Do you think he robbed Windsor Castle?" Maria said under her breath.

Sarah had to restrain herself from laughing. "It is entirely possible. Look at the chandelier."

It was much too big for the space and the height of the ceiling. In fact, she wouldn't be surprised if she could touch it, if she stretched out her arm enough.

Maria was not so careful of giving a good impression and she let out a little gasp. Her eyes twinkled in amusement.

"I do believe we shall be able to keep ourselves occupied exploring this house for weeks," she said.

Sarah nodded. How her family would be entertained by her description of the house. She would write to her father, since she wasn't sure her mother wouldn't just throw her letter in the fire without even reading it.

The drawing room was thankfully nothing shocking. A well-sized room furnished with appropriate furniture. Two couches and a chaise were arranged around the fireplace. A desk was positioned by the window, with a pretty prospect of the garden outside.

It was at this desk that William Thorne had been sitting just moments before they entered. He was now standing and gave both of them a bow in greeting. A stiff politeness about him.

"Welcome to Oakham. I hope your journey was smooth."

It should have been Sarah as the senior in rank and age to reply, but she found herself caught off guard. So Maria had come to her rescue.

"Thank you, it was," Maria said.

"You are most kind to receive us. I am grateful you agreed to my entirety," Sarah said, finding her words.

He seemed to be considering Maria for a moment before turning that sharp gaze of his back to her.

"Hardly much I could do. You could claim your rights to living here. So I thought I'd save us both the trouble of going through lawyers."

She had to keep from saying the first thing that came into her head, which was neither kind nor very ladylike of her.

"I am sorry if that is how you feel. It was not my intention to be an imposition on you, sir," Sarah said, imitating his coldness. She felt the exhaustion of her journey hit her. She wasn't sure what she had been expecting when she arrived, but it wasn't to jump into an argument right away.

Wasn't this why she had left home?

At least he didn't hold the same sway over her as her parents did. Nor did she feel she had to curb her tongue as much.

"You wrote in your letter that there was a cottage that Sir Ralph had been converting into a guest house. I had assumed I would be taking up residence there."

He was looking down at the letters on his desk and looked up at her words.

"Yes, I am sure you will find it adequate."

"Then I shall have my things moved there immediately, so I do not intrude upon your goodness any longer."

He seemed taken aback by her words.

"It is a long walk from the house. You might as well stay, and we can go and see it tomorrow," he said at last.

Sarah got the feeling he was talking to her as though she was a child. Something she did not appreciate.

"Then we would be grateful for a tour of your beautiful home." Maria jumped in to save the situation.

Sarah threw her a look, knowing that her friend had ulterior motives rather than simply changing the subject. If he knew her any better, then he would know that Maria could be quite nefarious indeed.

As it stood he seemed to welcome the idea.

"A splendid idea," he said, setting down his pen.

"I have been able to start getting together a list of projects that need to be completed around the house. I know it is in a state of disrepair, and the furnishings are not quite to my taste."

An image of the chandelier popped into her mind, and Sarah had to work hard to keep her expression steady.

"Ah, so half-finished roads aren't the latest fashion?" Maria teased.

Thorne surprised her by laughing. It was a pleasant, deep sound that seemed to reverberate in his chest.

"Not to my knowledge. I hope it didn't give you ladies discomfort. My cousin, when he bought this estate, had many plans for improving it. You see, it had been left in disrepair."

"And the cottage?" Sarah looked up, meeting his stormy grey eyes. "Is it liveable?"

He nodded. "I was considering moving in there

myself while work on the house is completed, but nothing to fear; you may have it. I am tired of fighting fate."

Her lips turned up in a sort of half-smile.

Why did he always seem to get so defensive whenever she spoke? Maybe she should use Maria as an intermediary. Was there some way she could convince her to stay indefinitely?

Before they could make any further plans, he invited them to sit down for a light meal.

"I am not sure when you last ate, but I am sure the journey was long, having made it myself," he said with a smile.

The dining room was nicely laid out with plates and cutlery. She wasn't sure what she expected, having never been to the home of a bachelor; however, she attributed this to the housekeeper, unable to imagine that he would bother with such things as napkin rings.

The three-course meal featured a clear soup, roasted vegetables, and chicken, as well as a fruit compote served over toast. It was lovely and filling. Just what the two of them needed.

"Shall we have tea, or would you like the tour now?"

"Oh, let's have the tour!" Maria said, eager now that she had been fed.

Sarah nodded her head in agreement.

He led the way, starting back at the main entrance.

"As you can see, some changes need to be made here..." he said, his gaze settling on the chandelier. "But there are other pressing matters to attend to. If you will step right this way."

He opened up a doorway to the right of the house. Sarah could see what he meant immediately. There had obviously been a fire here recently that had blackened the walls along the fireplace and even the ceiling. The old wallpaper was already mostly stripped away.

"We shall have to replaster the walls and cover it with something suitable, but this should be a nice room. There is a beautiful prospect of the park, through the large window over there," Thorne said, pointing over.

Sarah bravely marched through, not worrying about the dust on the floor. Her dress already was in need of a good washing.

He was right. She could see a beautiful willow tree and a little pond even. It was a pleasant aspect. She could have imagined that this would be a room she would spend a lot of time in. Not that she would be, of course.

He took them through the rest of the house. There were eight bedrooms upstairs, although two of them were quite small. A drawing room, a library with a door just off it that led to an office on the main floor. The office had its floorboards pulled out and were in the process of repair as well, explaining why he was working in the drawing room—a small assembly room that might be large enough to host a small party, though maybe not a ball...but perhaps. It would be easier to judge when the room wasn't being used as storage, as many of the rooms had been in need of great repair.

Overall, though, she could see the potential. She would have been horrified to arrive here as a new bride.

She wondered when Sir Ralph would have thought it was necessary to inform her.

She complimented him honestly on every aspect that she could find worthy of praise. Sarah supposed she was trying to butter him up to improve his view of her. They would be working together after all, as she had forced herself into his company.

If the cottage was indeed far enough that she couldn't reach it comfortably today, then she supposed they could avoid being together even if they decided to hate each other.

Could she isolate herself for the rest of her life? She supposed she could if she had a decent library.

"My niece will be joining me to keep house for me. It was always my intention to have her live with me, despite hiring my admirable housekeeper, but with your arrival I thought it would be even more prudent."

Sarah bit her lower lip. He had gone to some trouble then, it seemed, to accommodate her.

She was about to open her mouth to say something. Maybe apologize, but he seemed to know what she was about to say and held up a hand.

"Don't trouble yourself with apologies. I know this is your right as my cousin's widow. My niece is currently without a home of her own as her husband has taken up a naval command. When he returns in a year, he will retire from the navy and they shall settle down somewhere more permanent."

"Your poor niece. She must be very lonely without

her husband. How generous of you to look after her," Maria said.

She said this with such genuine feeling that Sarah had to look twice at her. Maria had often joked about finding William handsome, but was there some actual truth to this? Sarah couldn't help but frown. Her friend was so adamant against marriage that she doubted this. She argued with herself that it was just because she was in a good mood, but she wasn't sure.

Finally, they retired to a room. Sarah said she wouldn't mind sharing, since it seemed they were short on space. She also wouldn't mind the chance to pick her friend's brain.

They had eaten another meal, before bed, and had tea. William Thorne had left them in the hands of his housekeeper, Mrs. Adams. She was an amiable woman of a friendly disposition, despite the stern expression she wore.

"My mother says it was a tumble I took that made my face freeze this way. To be honest with you, I got so used to squinting that now it looks like I am permanently frowning. By the time someone suggested I needed spectacles to see better it was too late. Here I go, rambling on about myself," Mrs. Adams said as she set down the tea service. "Please don't hesitate to ask me for anything. I assume you have not brought your own cook? I shall put out an advertisement for you in the newspaper if you wish."

Sarah, who had not thought of this, was grateful.

"I am sure the master would not mind you eating

your meals here, or your man can fetch up a few dishes for you."

"I wouldn't want to put them to any trouble," Sarah said, feeling her face begin to grow hot.

"Nonsense, Lady Askew," the housekeeper said with a grin. "You cannot make the walk over three times a day."

"Lady Askew will surprise you," Maria said, chiming in as she accepted a cup of tea from her. "She will be stubborn about sacrificing herself only to avoid annoying others."

Sarah looked away from the inquisitive gaze of the housekeeper.

"Well, I cannot help my nature."

"See how she apologizes?" Maria laughed. "We must cure her of it. If she is to be a mistress."

Mrs. Adams seemed to agree with her, but Sarah knew it would be fruitless to argue with her friend. She mused how grateful she had been for her friend's presence at the beginning of this trip and wondered if this was now changing.

As promised, the very next day they set out for the cottage.

Mr. Thorne led the way, carrying a walking stick in case there were any overgrown bushes or plants encroaching on the path.

"This too I shall have fixed," he said over his shoulder to her.

"You shall have to send me the bill," Sarah said, not wishing him to think that she wouldn't be paying her own way.

"I will see to it immediately," he said, as though that had been his plan all along. She frowned.

Eventually, they would have to sit down and have a proper discussion about money. She knew she would be paying her own way, but some things would have to be shared. She did not think she had the budget to keep her own carriage, but perhaps he wouldn't mind sharing his own if she helped pay for the maintenance. She would like her own horse, though, as she enjoyed riding from time to time.

The land around here seemed beautiful and flat, perfect for long walks and rides if she was inclined. She tried to refocus her attention; there would be more serious matters for her to attend to, not just thinking of how she might amuse herself.

"Here we are," he said. "Just over this little ridge."

The top of the ridge revealed a valley.

The path wound its way down. Sarah looked puzzled. How big was the land they lived on? Was this a farmer's cottage?

She could see now why he had suggested that she wait until morning to come see her new home.

Maria could feel her apprehension and gave her hand a little squeeze.

As they came closer, it was clear the building seemed

sturdy, with a tiled roof and whitewashed walls with ivy climbing up them. The window shutters were painted a striking red.

"I am told the previous owner installed his ailing mother here. She had a love of red. Hence the roses in the garden as well," he said, pointing to them. "They are all over the estate actually. Growing faster than weeds."

"Why was this land left in such a...condition?" she asked for lack of a better word.

He shrugged.

"Why would Sir Ralph buy it?"

He whipped his head around, staring at her pointedly. "You should know, as his grieving widow."

Sarah avoided his gaze, unable to bear his reproof or the intensity of his gaze.

Maria was quick to rise to her defence. "You should know as his cousin and heir. You have known him for much longer. Why would a man share his thoughts with a woman?"

Sarah was grateful, though she wished she didn't need such a friend to stand up to the likes of William Thorne, who was proving to be nothing better than a bully.

He looked away from them both.

"I shall have someone bring your things here and see you settled in. The cottage is furnished, and anything you want to change you may."

"Mrs. Adams said she was putting in an advertisement for a cook for me. In the meantime, I will be having meals at the house..." She paused; this was coming out wrong. "What I mean to say is, if that is not too much of an inconvenience."

He looked exasperated, his eyes looking off into the far distance as he pinched the bridge of his nose.

"It had occurred to me you had come with a very small household. Even the manservant is not to stay with you, is that correct?"

She nodded, looking abashed.

"Nothing that cannot be remedied," Maria said, once again chiming in.

They had begun taking the path down the lane, but Thorne seemed keen on getting down faster and walked straight down the hillside. Sarah knew she had been mistaken, but she had thought it wouldn't be such a trouble to hire local help and, in the meantime, make use of the servants he had already hired. What would be so wrong in that?

But of course, she had failed to be clear. Unable to find the correct words, and now she had made an even bigger mess.

"Sarah, you can't go on like this," Maria said, prodding her.

"I failed to plan properly. Even though I thought I had. I was simply thinking of the expense and of the fact I did not want to pull anyone away from their home. Why uproot someone?"

"You always think of others and try not to be an inconvenience to anyone, don't you?"

"Well...yes."

"Don't you see how that can land you in more trouble?"

"Please don't be frustrated with me. I cannot stand two disappointed people," Sarah said, some real desperation in her voice.

A sigh from her dark friend. "You know I will always defend you."

Sarah smiled. "Not sure how I tricked you into doing that. The last few months took a bizarre turn, and I couldn't have seen how to prepare. You know I am usually very rational. I helped take over many of my mother's duties back at home."

"You are right. So I will forgive this lapse in judgement," Maria said, giving her a wide smile. "Look what a pretty prospect your new home makes. I must set to sketching it before I leave."

Sarah looked up and saw the wooden fence intertwined with rose bushes. The red buds ready to flower. She could see the effect would be stunning.

The cottage itself was quite imposing when faced with it close up.

Thorne had unlocked the front door and held it open for them.

"I had the servants clean up a few days ago. But the air might still be a bit stale. Before Sir Ralph took possession of this place it had not been in use for several months," he said by way of explanation.

"The mystery grows," Sarah said, with what she hoped was a pleasant smile.

The cottage's greatest advantage was large

windows. She hoped this did not mean that it would be very cold at night or in the depths of winter. The parlour was of a decent size and even featured a drawing room at the back. Upstairs there were three bedrooms.

Everything seemed to be in decent order and, more importantly, clean.

It seemed as though Sir Ralph had not touched this building with his own renovations or tastes in furniture.

The pair of them explored every alcove and opened every door, even venturing into the kitchen and out the back door to an overgrown herb garden that could be dug up quite easily.

"Oh look, you have peppermint," Maria pointed out. "We must have tea here this afternoon."

Sarah agreed with her wholeheartedly.

A breeze picked up then, and she took a deep breath, enjoying the scent of fresh air, grass, and herbs all intermingled.

"I could definitely be happy here," she said.

"I am happy to hear that," a voice said from behind her, making Sarah jump.

"I did not mean to startle you. I thought you knew I had come too." Thorne looked apologetic.

Sarah blushed; she hadn't meant for him to hear that.

Maria was looking from one to the other with amusement.

"Will you join us for tea here then?"

He looked a bit surprised by the invitation.

"You shall of course have to supply the provisions,

but we could whip up a pleasant picnic out here," Maria said.

Sarah wondered where she got her haughtiness from. She placed a hand on her friend's wrist as though to stop her.

"If I am not otherwise occupied," he replied, after a moment's hesitation.

The corner of Sarah's lip twitched. Had he tried to think of an excuse and couldn't think of one? She was amused to learn that he wasn't as sharp-witted as he had seemed to be at first.

True to their word, they arranged the picnic with the housekeeper. Some essentials were already stocked in their kitchen, and a kitchen maid had come to prepare the tea and snacks.

"I shall send Dorothy to stay with you. We can spare her for a day or two, and we shall have you make a list of some of your favourite things and I'll send for things from the market."

Sarah didn't know how to thank her.

"No need, my dear. It is my job. You would have come to this house a new bride, and you should have seen the state of the house before Mr. Thorne got his hands on it. God forgive me for saying this, but he did more in a week than Sir Ralph Askew did in five," Mrs. Adams said with a wink.

"Not all men are so eager for such tasks. He spoke to

me of wishing that I would oversee the setting up of our house." Sarah felt safe confiding in her.

Mrs. Adams' expression dropped. "Pardon me, Lady Askew. I should not have spoken ill of the dead. It was highly improper."

"No. It was the truth, I am sure. I am glad that Mr. Thorne is doing a good job taking care of my late husband's estate. I am sure he would be happy to know it is all looked after," she said, forcing herself to smile.

It was often that she forgot exactly this very thing herself. She might be dressed as a widow with her cap and black dresses, but she hardly felt like one. She supposed a year would fly by sooner than she thought, then she could wear something that did not make her look so severe and austere.

Thorne arrived punctually at three o'clock.

They had set out a few blankets and cushions on the grass. Maria had her sketchbook out.

The maid and kitchen maid brought out the tray of cakes and tea.

They enjoyed a nice conversation, talking about the village and neighbours. He told her of his plans for the house and the land. She hadn't given much thought to the farm and what he would plan to grow. He wanted to convert half the fields to pasture for cows.

"I was looking over the records, and I think I could squeeze more profit out of the land if we did that."

"We?" Her eyebrow arched.

"Well...yes, to some degree," he said, biting into a

cake. "Our fortunes are tied up together now, but I shall manage it well."

She gave him a challenging look. "How do I know you are capable, sir?"

He nearly choked on his cake. Even Maria chuckled.

Sarah was mortified and wanted to jump to her feet and run inside. She schooled herself, though she couldn't keep from biting her lip.

"Forgive me, I did not mean to say that. It came out all wrong."

"I can vouch for her," Maria said.

Thorne looked more amused than insulted, and Sarah watched as he popped the last of the cake into his mouth.

"Never fear, madam. I shall send you my credentials," he said, with an exaggerated bow of his head.

Her face became even more heated, and she had likely turned a red similar to that of the shutters.

"You cannot tease her, or she will have a case of the vapours," Maria warned, turning her attention back to her sketchbook.

Sarah was ready to disappear. Maybe the ground would decide to open up and swallow her.

"Don't fret," Thorne said at last. "You are right to worry about that. It might not be polite, but this is both our futures that we have to worry about. If either of us invests poorly, we lose our livelihoods and we will be cast out on the street. I do hate some social conventions."

"Thank you for saying so," Sarah said, recovering her

spirits. "I often find myself at odds with what society expects of me."

"I find that unlikely," he said as though it was an afterthought he hadn't meant to say out loud.

The rest of their little picnic passed without incident.

They spoke a bit more about his plans, and Sarah promised him she would get her house in order and would not impose on him.

"You shall have to occasionally force yourself to come out from your refuge," he said from the cottage door.

For a second there she thought he was trying to imply he was eager for her company, but then he continued.

"My niece has a very social nature, and I daresay she will be calling on you and expecting you to return the favour as soon as she arrives. Upon you as well, Miss Clement," he added, turning to Maria.

"As long as I am here. I was given leave to stay for a fortnight but no longer."

"A pity we shall see you leave so soon." He bowed to them both and bade them farewell.

Sarah watched him disappear over the ridge before closing the door.

She turned to her friend with a sheepish grin on her face.

"I do believe he likes you."

"What?" Maria seemed surprised. "Hardly."

Sarah's eyebrows twitched in amusement. "A pity, he says." She threw her hand up dramatically as though she might swoon.

"He is right though," she added. "It will be a pity

when you leave. If I did not have my reservations about him then I would suggest you set your cap at him. He would be a good match, and even better, we would be so very close to one another. I could be the nursemaid to all your darling little children."

Maria looked disgusted at the prospect.

"I wouldn't mind you as a constant companion, but I could do without all the rest," Maria said.

"I do have one more favour to ask of you, dearest friend," Sarah said, batting her eyelashes.

"What?"

"Allow me the pleasure of seeing you reject him when he does propose."

Sarah laughed at her friend's expression.

"You might joke all you want at my expense, but beware of what you say. It might come back to bite you."

Sarah could tell she had taken the joke too far.

"I am sorry, I am teasing. Any man would be lucky to have you, on that I am serious. But the real favour I would ask of you is to deliver my letters to my family when you go. I am sure they are worried about me but, seeing as you are just as likely to arrive there as soon as the post would, I would prefer you to carry it for me."

Maria obliged her and agreed.

They spent much of their first week at the cottage arranging the things she had brought with her and moving around the furniture to suit her needs and style.

They also explored as much of the land surrounding Oakham as they dared. Sarah knew their solitude could not last long. Surely there were neighbours who would be curious enough to pay them a call.

But, seeing the state of the main house, she wouldn't be surprised if Thorne had put off any potential callers. He also didn't seem to be the type to befriend everyone, but that was unfair. After all, he had come to spend the afternoon with them and did not begrudge her any help when she needed it.

Sarah would have to forgive his behaviour towards her before. Could she truly blame him for not jumping for joy that she had come to claim her dower home? What if he had plans of his own to marry and set up a house here? Had she muddled things for him? She didn't know him well enough to bring it up, but she hoped the niece would be of some help in this matter.

She was sure she could find another comfortable home somewhere else if he preferred and was too polite to have told her no.

CHAPTER FIVE

Sarah was finishing up a letter to her parents when she heard a knock at the door.

Her maid answered it and, a few moments later, came to see her with a note.

"It's from the house. The manservant is waiting for a reply," she said, handing her the note.

Maria looked intrigued but tried her best not to be nosy.

Sarah unfolded it and read aloud.

"'Good morning. My niece is set to arrive, and I was hoping you might do us the honour of joining us for breakfast tea tomorrow morning. I am sure she would enjoy the company.'"

"Ah, the infamous niece. Of course we shall go," Maria said with a smile, before turning back to her book.

Sarah wondered if it was another one of her secret books, as she was so engrossed in it.

"I'll add something quickly in the postscript." She

walked over to her little writing desk and wrote out a hasty reply.

The maid took it and was gone.

"I am curious to meet her," Maria said, looking up from her book. "I wonder if she will be absolutely intolerable and you will be begging to come back with me."

"Imagine if I were to do that? I am sure my mother would be very pleased to see that she was proven correct."

"Your mother is hardly ever correct. You are finally free of needing her permission or even her good opinion," Maria pointed out.

Sarah couldn't help scolding her. "She's my mother and I love her dearly. Faults and all. I cannot claim to know any better than she does."

Maria scoffed but, knowing she would get no further, did not bring up the matter again.

As they were shown into the house, Sarah could hear the distant sound of a woman's voice exclaiming over every little thing.

"Will, this is quite a beautiful piece," she heard as they waited for the footman to announce them.

The voice grew quiet.

They strode in side by side and were greeted with the sight of a very tall but beautiful woman. She could not have been much older than they were, though her countenance and air gave her a feeling of maturity neither Sarah nor Maria yet possessed.

Her expression broke into a warm smile as she saw the pair of them.

"I have heard so much about you both," she said, not giving them or Thorne much time for introductions.

Thorne came forward and made the proper introductions.

Sarah was amused but grateful to see that such a flamboyant, talkative woman would be residing at Oakham with them. If it was left to her and Thorne, they would become hermits in a matter of months.

They learned with some swiftness that Eloise Haverstock was in the family way. It was early days, but her husband had forbidden her from travelling with him or camping out near a seaport.

"It is better you came here," Thorne said, after she had finished complaining bitterly.

"How can I be expected to live so far away from him?"

"It is not safe...if there were to be an invasion."

She laughed, waving the thought away as though it was the silliest of ideas.

"They say Napoleon is distracted with the Egyptians," Eloise claimed.

Sarah watched the exchange with some amusement.

"At least I will get to play house while I am here. I cannot believe the state of this place. If Charles saw it he would sneak me on board his ship." Eloise tutted. "At least this room is in decent condition."

Even Maria was taken aback by her exuberance, but everyone was put at ease by her easy manner and conversation.

They ate well, enjoying a cheerful discourse. Despite their plans being limited to lunch they did not leave until well after supper.

"She is quite the character," Sarah said to Maria as they entered her cottage to find that a fire was burning in the grate. It was a chilly night, and she would be more than happy to warm herself by the fire for a while.

Days passed by in easy succession. Maria was to leave soon, and this left Sarah in a sour, nervous sort of mood. She tried not to let her feelings show, especially because she was so grateful to Maria for accompanying her this far.

Maria was in no urgency to go, but her mother demanded her return.

"What will become of me once I return?" she said, lamenting her fate.

"Your mother is more understanding than mine," Sarah said. "Besides, I shall be back for Christmas."

"I am sure you will be delayed somehow."

Sarah frowned. "I would not delay a Christmas with my family even if I was married."

"Maybe your Mr. Thorne will contrive to keep you here forever," Maria said with that grin of hers. She had taken delight in vexing her.

"You know I hate it when you tease me about him. I am sure he hates me rather than anything even close to love. So you can stop implying things. Of the two of us I think you have the better chance with him," she said.

"At what?"

Sarah froze mid-step. They were walking in the garden, under a shaded alcove that hugged the main house.

Together, they turned around.

Maria had the falsest of smiles pasted on her face. Sarah could tell she too was trying to hide her embarrassment and discomfort.

"At convincing you to throw a ball," Maria said, thinking of the first thing that came to mind.

William Thorne looked doubtful. Sarah said a silent prayer that this would be believable.

"I told her the house is in no state for a ball," Sarah explained. "To which she replied, then surely a garden party to meet the neighbours would be perfectly acceptable. What do you think? Am I right in assuming this would not be appealing to you?"

This seemed to calm his suspicions, and he seemed to consider the request.

"It would be the prudent thing to introduce myself to the neighbours. I have paid them a few calls but have not been the most amiable of neighbours, largely due to the issues on the estate. I shall talk to the workers and see when the road might be complete. You may have your garden party after all."

"See, Sarah, he is perfectly amenable to your

suggestions," Maria said, taking her hand. "Mr. Thorne, you must assure my friend of your good opinion of her. She is certain that you dislike her very much."

"Maria," Sarah snapped at her, pulling her arm away.

Maria was ignoring her and giving Thorne a challenging look.

"I am sorry I have given you that impression, Lady Askew," he said, his expression twisted in what Sarah might call a combination of surprise and frustration.

"No...Miss Clement misspoke. I am very grateful for all you have done for me. You have been more than kind and considerate." She rushed to assure him that she wasn't resentful of him and did not wish to give him the impression she wanted more from him.

"I shall leave you ladies to your walk," he said, beginning to turn around before remembering something. "Ah, I came to tell you that Eloise wanted to join you for dinner; if that is acceptable, I will relay the message. She is currently resting in her room."

"Of course," Sarah replied, more than happy for her company.

"Good." He hesitated a moment longer and was gone.

The two women let out a laugh when he was safely out of earshot.

"I thought I would die of embarrassment," Maria admitted. "You were quick on your feet, which is a good thing."

"I always rolled my eyes when my mother scolded us to be seen and not heard," Sarah said with a laugh. "I finally understand why that was actually sound advice."

"Yes, it turns out we have a thing or two we could learn from them." Maria gave a snort. "Well, I am happy to have many stories to tell when I go home. The visit was short, but not short of events."

"Maria, you cannot tell anyone."

Maria gave her a smile but did not promise.

They took the long walk back to the cottage to change and make it back in time for dinner.

Sarah's household had been furnished with the staff it needed, and an account had been set up for her at the local market. Her favourite part of the week was planning out the meals. She loved finally having a say in what was being served that day. Her mother always preferred heavy foods, laden with sauces. Now that she was master of her domain, so to speak, she could eat exactly what she pleased.

Of all things, this was probably one of her favourite things about being a widow.

Her wardrobe had extended to another dress; this one was a very dark navy blue. She thought it would be suitable enough, especially in the evening. The embroidery was very fine and the same colour as the fabric. It had been an extravagant expense, but she had been pleased to buy something for herself and to be able to send back that horrid dress to her mother.

During the day she took the chance to wear some of her older gowns. She was careful to choose dull, sombre colours, to not give rise to any talk or gossip about her. She was just tired of looking so ghostly.

Her year of mourning would be at an end faster than

she thought—at least that's what everyone kept telling her.

Mrs. Rodes, the parson's wife, came to pay her respects, one of the first and only people to do so.

The parish had seen very little of Sir Ralph Askew; many had not even seen him in person.

She had seemed surprised to find Sarah installed in such great comfort but of such a young age. When she had begun nosing about the particulars of the arrangement, Sarah had been quick to shut down the conversation. No one needed to know and least of all this nosy woman.

She was beginning to think she was the village gossip the way she fished for information. Though was that surprising? It often happened that in a village as small as this one, with fewer than twelve gentile families, there was little news and little to talk about.

Still, Sarah had been polite and offered to invite her for tea to introduce her to Eloise, who was keeping house for her uncle.

"What a peculiar arrangement you all have," Mrs. Rodes said.

"I do not find it so," Sarah replied. For once Maria had remained as silent as a lamb. Though from her fiery expression it was clear what she thought of the parson's wife.

"Very unusual. You should remarry and live away from here," she said. "Your parents should have kept you at home."

Sarah felt the need to correct her. "It is my father who recommended I take up an independent living."

This made her eyebrows shoot up.

"How interesting. Who is your father, Lady Askew?" she asked with such sweetness in her tone that Sarah felt nauseous.

"My family name is Barnette."

She hadn't given his full name; she wouldn't make it easy for this woman to do her snooping. However, seeing how her eyes lit up, she did not believe this would be much of a hindrance.

"I do believe is it Mr. Thorne's intention to throw a garden party sometime soon. I do apologize for the state of the house at present, as well as the road. I trust it will be put into repair shortly," Sarah said, indicating as politely as she could that it was time to go.

She attended church every Sunday along with Eloise, Maria, and William. They made quite the sight. Many comments had flown about until the relationship between all of them was made explicitly clear.

"Perhaps I should start calling you Aunt," Thorne had said.

She didn't know why this had caused her to go red.

"Please do not," she had said, her voice coming out in a half-whisper.

He had flashed her a rare smile.

"It does seem preposterous to think about but not as uncommon as you think. I had a stepbrother for a time old enough to be my own father."

"You did?"

"Yes, my mother was notorious for remarrying. She was married at least four times during my lifetime. I could say she had a stroke of bad luck." He laughed to himself.

She looked at him questioningly.

"Two of those husbands died of strokes."

"How tragic," she said, unable to imagine what that must have been like for her.

"Well, look at it this way. She fell easily in and out of love, then after a time she made prudent matches to ensure I was well looked after."

"It still must have caused quite a stir among your relations.'

"Perhaps it did, but at least she didn't end up in the newspapers," he said with a far-off look. "She lived to a good age. She had me quite late in life. I think I was a surprise to her."

"Then I suppose I am just unfortunate that I did end up being spoken about in every corner of the empire."

He seemed to stop mid-step, realizing what he had said.

"Now it is my turn to apologize," he said, with a cough. "I realize it must have been very hard for you to have such a private matter laid bare before the world."

She smiled, genuinely pleased that he had expressed such kindness towards her.

"I appreciate it. I must be frank with you. It was hard for me to endure such public embarrassment," she said. "It was not that I did not care for your cousin...I readily agreed to marry him and had hoped to enjoy a long life together. I did not know him as someone ought to know their spouse, so when he passed so suddenly, I was caught off guard. I did not know what to do, but I supposed I wanted to ensure my safety. It was aggravated by the fact I seemed to become such a social pariah overnight. No one except my dear Maria wanted to associate with me after that. It was..." she paused, trying to collect herself before she divulged every bit of her heart to him, "...a difficult time. Made worse by my mother's insistence on shutting me away."

His expression was grave. "This is the most I have heard you speak since the meeting with the lawyer. I must confess I had found it...peculiar, how you had presumably gone into mourning tucked away in your rooms. I found it hard to imagine you were in there crying your heart out. Or that you wished for the world to think you were."

Sarah shook her head. "Heavens, no. I hadn't even considered how ridiculous that must have seemed, and then when I did come out, I was decked head-to-toe in that hideous black frilly gown."

His lips twitched in amusement. "I had noticed."

A laugh escaped her. "I am glad we can be honest with each other now. Please do tell me when I am at risk of seeming ridiculous again."

He regarded her with an almost caring expression.

"I shall do my very best," he said.

They went their separate ways after that, Sarah choosing to join Maria as she sketched another landscape.

"I shall try to paint them from memory when I get home. I forgot my watercolours," Maria said, showing her the pictures.

Sarah peered closer to see that she had drawn two figures walking hand in hand down the pretty lane. She frowned.

"Is that—"

"You? Yes," Maria said, a challenging grin on her face.

"Dare I ask who the person is beside me?"

"If you wish," Maria said, a playful coyness to her voice.

"I shall ignore your childish games," Sarah said with finality.

This was the one time during her whole visit that Sarah found herself wishing Maria was not there. It was a source of embarrassment and felt too much like the sort of speculation she had experienced from her elders. She had always avoided certain parties for this very reason. Why should she have to account for her every action? It was hard enough trying to find a way around her new life. She hoped Maria was the only one speculating about her "budding" relationship with William. If it could be called that. The fact that they had begun to tolerate each other's presence was hardly the foundation of a budding romance.

But she could see Maria's point—people jumped to conclusions.

~

Even in the short time since she had arrived it seemed as though the house was slowly transforming itself. The cobblestones had been brought in and workmen were continuing the path started all those months ago.

It was starting to look like a proper house.

A small team of apprentices were brought in to begin tackling the gardens and even the ivy clinging to the walls. She enjoyed talking to them about the work they were doing.

She hoped next spring to start a lovely little herb garden of her own. Sarah knew she would need work to keep her occupied.

Maria's date of departure was barely a day away. She helped her friend pack with great reluctance. She would be losing her greatest ally, not to mention friend.

"Are we to have supper at the main house?" Maria asked, as she put the last of her things in the trunk.

"No, I thought we could enjoy our own company. Maybe take one last stroll around the grounds together. I did say we would join them for breakfast tomorrow before you leave," Sarah said. "If you do not like my plan, then just let me know and I am sure they would accommodate you. Eloise seemed to take a liking to you."

Maria waved away her concerns. "It shall be good to spend an evening in quiet contemplation." She was mimicking the sermon they had heard that morning in church. The parson's booming voice had seemed both monotone yet overly dramatic for the sermon he was preaching to the congregation; only his wife had seemed enraptured.

"You must come and visit again soon," Eloise said; real tears were in her eyes and she kept wiping them away. "I blame the pregnancy for being so emotional. Pardon me."

"Nothing to apologize for. I am sad to see that my friend has not yet shed a tear." Maria looked at Sarah with reproof.

"They have all been spent." Sarah gave her a smile. It was true she had shed quite a few tears over the last few months, so it wasn't surprising that her eyes were dry now. Though a general sense of melancholy had settled over her.

"You shall try to send the letters on to my parents as soon as you can?"

"I promise."

Now that Sarah had been away from home for a while, she found herself growing more homesick by the hour. She had to constantly remind herself this was for the best. This was what she wanted and what many people dreamed of. Her father had said she had a shrewd mind; it was time for her to begin to think rationally and count her blessings.

Before Maria left, Sarah extracted another promise to visit soon.

"You shall have to come and see what I have done to the place once I am more settled. I might even be able to send you things from my herb garden."

"That would be lovely indeed. You should also see about getting a harpsichord. I am sure the drawing room could fit one comfortably," Maria said, then turned to Mr. Thorne. "Thank you for looking after my friend. I do hope you will ask her to play for you one of these days. She does play beautifully, though she is incredibly shy about it."

"Maria, must you..."

Eloise broke the silence with a twinkling laugh.

"The pair of you act like such loving sisters. But I will promise on Mr. Thorne's behalf that we shall have dearest Sarah play for us."

Maria smiled. The carriage had arrived, and she gave Sarah one last embrace.

"Take care of yourself, and don't be too prudish," she said, a flash of mischief in her eye.

"Maria, this isn't some romance novel. I really do think you should stop reading them; they are corrupting you." Sarah was joking as well.

"I am incorrigible, as my mother often assures me. Take care. I hope to hear from you soon and regularly," Maria said and gave a curtsey to the others waiting at the door before allowing herself to be helped up the steps of the carriage by Mr. Thorne.

Sarah mused that he could be such a gentleman when he wanted to. It was a pity he wasn't usually so amiable.

She stood in the doorway waving to her friend until the carriage was out of sight, and then stayed a further moment breathing in the autumn air. The season was changing. What was to become of her?

As though sensing her mood, Eloise pulled her away.

"You shall have to keep me company every day. I insist."

Sarah made an effort to seem cheerful.

"That is very kind of you. I wouldn't wish to impose."

"Nonsense. Besides, playing at cards with three is much more enjoyable. I cannot wait to start accepting invitations on my uncle's behalf. He still insists that we do not go out into society as the house is not yet ready to receive visitors. Men can be so infuriating." Eloise went on rambling.

William Thorne proved to be immune to his niece's requests to accept invitations. Sarah was surprised to find how he doted on his niece. They were more like friends, but she supposed he took his charges seriously and wanted to ensure she was looked after while her husband was away.

They enjoyed a lovely morning together. Sarah helped Eloise while she worked on painting a screen, and she read to her from a book of poetry.

Mr. Thorne was still using the drawing room as his office and was working away.

She caught him stopping from time to time and worried that she was distracting him.

"Shall I stop? Please don't worry about hurting my feelings; I would not wish to keep your from your work," Sarah said, unable to stop herself.

"No, please continue. It is a pleasant contrast to the usual silence."

"I've never been a great reader but I enjoy listening to you. It is the same with music. I enjoy listening to others but hate playing the piano myself," Eloise said, as though admitting a shameful secret.

"Despite my friend's praises, I do not play quite so well as I should. My mother spent a fortune on piano teachers, even took me to London for a season, but I never improved much." Sarah found it easy to open up to Eloise who seemed to soak in all the gossip like a sponge.

"At least your mother did not give up on you. Speaking of which," she said, turning to William at the desk, "my mother wrote to me she wishes to join us for Christmas. I thought that would be acceptable. Even if I am not here any longer. We can make it a new family tradition for, despite its flaws, this is still the finest house in our family."

Sarah thought she had caught the hint of a blush on his cheeks. Thorne was not used to being affluent it seemed.

"Hopefully those flaws shall be rectified by then. That sounds pleasant though. And you, Lady Askew? Are you to stay for Christmas?"

She shook her head. "I would not dare impose myself in such a way. I have promised that I would travel back and visit my old home until after the New Year."

"I can make arrangements for you," he said.

"No, you do not need to. I will look into it. You've done so much already; there's no need for you to do even more," she said with a shy smile. "I must learn to stand on my own two feet. As my friend would say if she was here."

"Your friend is a very wise creature," Eloise said, then

called her attention to her work. "What do you think of this blue? I think it is a tad too dark."

Sarah looked away from Thorne and at the screen.

She was not invited to stay for lunch, but she had not minded as she was eager to see to things around the house. It was time she started a proper ledger to keep track of her expenses and make a few plans of her own now that she wasn't busy keeping Maria entertained.

For the next few days she stayed away from the main house, though Eloise had come to visit her and they sat outside enjoying the warm weather. A plum tree in her garden was nearly ripe to be harvested.

"You shall have to make jams and plenty of cakes with it. I love plums so very much," Eloise said, staring at them hungrily.

"I shall send you a basket as soon as they are ready," Sarah offered kindly. She herself did not care much for sweet foods, preferring savoury dishes instead.

"What are you writing?" Eloise asked, peering at her writing desk with some interest.

"A letter to Maria and another for my family. I am enclosing this little sketch for my sister, Louisa. She would enjoy running around here."

"How old is she?"

"She is just a little over twelve. I don't think she ever plans on growing up," Sarah said with a laugh.

"I don't think any of us ever want to."

Sarah looked at her, surprised. "I wouldn't have thought that of you."

Eloise had a wistful expression on her face. "It is much easier playing than actually experiencing it. When I played with my dolls and pretended to be their mother, I gave no thought to the aches and pains I would experience. They were also very quiet children," she said in a whisper.

Sarah laughed. "I know. I had my illusions dashed after the birth of my sister and then brother. I am the oldest by eight years, so you can imagine my surprise at how much noise an infant could produce. But they are sweet creatures."

Eloise seemed uncertain. "At least I shall have the best nursemaids for this little one. And if it is a girl, I'll dress her up in the latest fashions."

Sarah nodded. "Have you heard from your husband? I am sure he is eager to return to your side."

Eloise fixed her gaze on the horizon. "Yes, he is eager. I am happy here. I don't know what sort of home he has in mind for us, and he hardly takes me into account."

Seeing the questioning look from Sarah, she leaned closer and continued so no one might overhear. "I think he thinks I am quite silly and does not pay me much attention. I think the cleverest thing he thinks I did was conceive."

Sarah must have looked quite shocked because Eloise sat back, nodding.

"Yes, tragic I know. But we are quite happy in our

own way. He dotes on me. I just wish he didn't think I was a silly fool."

Sarah wondered why they had gotten married then, but it wasn't her place to ask. Already she was surprised that Eloise had confided so much in her.

She was distracted from her letters, and soon Eloise wished to head back to the house.

"I am glad you are here. I would have been very lonely here by myself."

"I thought you had come on my account," Sarah said with a frown.

"Oh, I contrived it that way. See, I am quite clever when it comes to it. My husband would have sent me home to my mother, but she lives in the most unfashionable part of town and I hate all the nosy relations we have. I would never have a moment's peace."

"I can sympathize," Sarah said, and bade her farewell.

She was a peculiar creature. Sarah wasn't quite sure what to make of Eloise Haverstock. Everything she said seemed to lead her to having five more questions. But from what she had gathered, she and William Thorne had not come from the most affluent of families. She knew more about Sir Ralph's side of the family than his. Thorne had been the son of his father's sister who had not made the most prudent marriage, and that was all he had said about the matter.

He had mostly talked about his plans and accomplishments during the time they had spoken. She herself had not been very interested in learning more about a man she had regarded so coldly at the time.

It was funny that fate had brought them together despite their seeming incompatibility.

At the end of the following week she was invited to dine with them for supper. Fortunately she had been too busy to notice the lack of visits she had received from Eloise despite the promise made on the day Maria departed.

Even as she walked up to the house she could see a great many changes had been made. The bushes had been trimmed back, and there was a beautiful paved road. Gone was the bumpy dirt path. She could now admire the cream stonework and the big windows without being distracted.

She was also pleased to see upon entering that the chandelier was gone. Replaced with another more modest one, but it made the entrance immediately look bigger and gave it a pleasant feel.

Eloise greeted her with a big smile.

"William has gone into town, so I thought we could be left in peace to plan out the little garden party," she said with true excitement in her tone.

Sarah smiled. "I would be more than happy to help. If you think that it is fine with him."

Eloise waved away her concern. "Of course. What would please a man more than to not have to think of such trivialities as planning a party. It will be good for you to socialize as well. You cannot keep yourself holed up in that cottage of yours."

I wouldn't have to if you invited me out, Sarah thought to herself, but she did not voice her opinion.

Eloise was likely just forgetful, as both her condition and general disposition seemed to make her. She would not hold this against her.

They sat down for a dinner of four courses, since Eloise had been unable to decide between a salad and soup before finally settling on having both. Then they retreated to the parlour, freshly wallpapered in a pale pink design.

Its overly feminine design made her think that Eloise had a hand in decorating. It was a good thing that she did not have any wild tastes like Sir Ralph had seemed to have. Everything, from the wallpaper to the furniture, was all done in good taste and comfortably arranged. It all seemed to be of the best quality and most fashionable fabrics. Thorne must have spent a tidy sum on all the changes.

"I made a list of everyone to invite." Eloise handed her a piece of paper. Her handwriting was neat and tidy with flowing letters that looked very elegant. A pang of envy struck her.

She looked over the list, recognizing some of the names from church but many others she did not know. Sarah regarded Eloise from underneath her lashes. Was she excluding her from visits? She couldn't imagine why this would be the case.

She put such thoughts out of her head. It was unkind of her and suspicious. When had she become so? Perhaps she too had been reading too many Gothic novels and was seeing plots everywhere.

There were a few names on the list that she knew could not be local.

"Are you inviting some of your own friends?" she asked, trying to sound as casual as possible.

Eloise looked up. "Yes, I thought it would even out the party a bit more, and I am sure William would enjoy seeing some of his old acquaintances."

Sarah looked back at the list. Most of these names were female. Had he been a ladies' man? She found that hard to believe; he seemed so averse to marriage in general.

They discussed a menu, and Eloise seemed happy enough for her input and scratched down a few of her suggestions.

"I'll make an arrangement of red roses. It will stand out so nicely against the white fabrics."

"You shall be needing my roses then," Sarah said, realizing what she was alluding to.

A wide toothy grin confirmed this. "You do have plenty, and I saw that the gardeners have not yet tackled your garden. You must have lots to spare. It's all for a good cause."

Sarah could not turn her down and agreed that she might have as many as she liked.

"You are such a good friend to me."

Sarah's heart warmed at her praise. She left shortly after they had settled on a general seating arrangement, and Eloise, quick with a pen, had sketched out what she was envisioning. This vision included a large tent that Sarah wasn't sure the house had in its possession yet.

"Don't worry, I will have William send out for one. This is his first party. It should be grand, otherwise what will people think? You must defend me if he complains. Do you promise?" Eloise said. She seemed to be working herself up into such a fit that Sarah was forced to agree.

She herself was too sensible to such a thing.

Sarah was busy helping to pick the plums off her tree in the small fenced-in garden the next day, when she spotted Mr. Thorne and Eloise strolling towards her arm in arm. She waved to them, and Eloise waved back.

"You must be terribly warm in your black dress," Eloise said as they approached.

It was indeed an unusually warm day. She used a handkerchief to wipe her face.

"It was for a good cause," she said, lifting her full basket for Eloise to see. Brimming with ripe plums.

She seemed pleased to see them.

"You must take them," Sarah said. "I know how you've been craving them."

Eloise thanked her, and even Mr. Thorne joined in praising her. "I am glad Eloise has someone to look after her so carefully."

Sarah nodded.

"Would you like to come in? I could call for some tea," she offered, taking off her gardener's gloves.

"Just passing through," Mr. Thorne said. "Eloise suggested she would enjoy a walk."

Sarah did not miss the mischievous expression that passed over Eloise's face.

"Yes, it seemed so nice outside. Now that we are here, we wanted to talk to you of the garden party."

"Ah." Mr. Thorne was knowledgeable enough to know when he had been trapped. "And?"

"Well, it would be lovely to hire some musicians for the party and have a tent set up. Sarah has already donated her lovely roses for the decor. This should be a lovely fête."

He frowned at her use of French but turned to Sarah with a look of surprise.

"You think this sort of extravagance is needed for a garden party?"

Sarah felt like she was caught in the middle between two warring parties, but she had already given her allegiance to one of them.

"It would be nice to start off on the right foot."

He frowned at her words, and she felt compelled to add, "If it isn't too much of an expense and I could help pay for it. It would only be right, since I am a resident on this estate."

Thorne looked between the two women and finally, with a shrug, agreed. "I shall send you my bill then. But this ought not to be repeated very often."

"How silly men are about money," Eloise said with a laugh. She was victorious and, ever affable, invited Sarah to join them for dinner that evening.

Sarah couldn't bring herself to meet Thorne's eyes,

feeling she had done something wrong and that his opinion of her now was forever tainted.

The very next Saturday Eloise sent out invitations to all the neighbours; printed on thick cardstock embossed with lace, it was as grand as a wedding invitation. Sarah had been quite taken aback by such extravagance.

"You shall be made the most fashionable of ladies in the neighbourhood by the time I am gone. I am surprised you would not have thought of it yourself. You seem so knowledgeable," Eloise said after Sarah had voiced her concerns.

"Yes, but I suppose my first concern would be the cost."

Eloise laughed. "You sound like my uncle. No one fashionable ever looks at money so closely."

"They might if they did not have much to spare."

Eloise pouted. "I am dreadfully sorry. Is it too much? I should have thought...well, it is too late."

Sarah forced herself to be conciliatory. After all, Eloise was young and had meant well.

This cheered the woman, and they enjoyed a pleasant conversation.

The next surprise had come when Sarah returned home after a luncheon to find her rose bushes stripped bare.

Her maid had looked at her with some pity, seeing her distress.

"The gardeners came when you were gone. They said you knew of the cutting."

"And so I did. I just didn't think they would take so much. I suppose a harsh pruning was in order anyway," Sarah said, her spirits deflated somewhat.

The next day, as she helped Eloise arrange the bouquets, she couldn't help but reprimand her for not being clear. This had reduced Eloise to tears, and William Thorne, who had been in the next room, came in to see what was wrong.

He had glared at Sarah so angrily that she had fled the house.

She sent a message to Eloise, apologizing and hoping she could make amends to her.

Eloise remained silent until the next day. She had apologized as well for making a scene, blaming her pregnancy.

"William says I have such a delicate constitution. He is always careful of me."

That was to imply that Sarah had not been. She pursed her lips but apologized profusely once more.

"Can I do anything to make it up to you?"

She regretted saying it the moment the words were past her lips, for Eloise's eyes lit up.

"Will you really? Because there is one thing. I greatly desire..."

"What is it?" Sarah couldn't help but smile. Her happiness was so infectious.

"There are these beautiful gloves I saw at the village store. White leather and oh so soft. Would you lend me the pocket money for them? I will be sure to repay you next month."

Sarah opened her mouth ready to agree but caught herself. "Why not get them next month then?"

Eloise's face fell, and Sarah found herself quickly reassuring her that she would purchase them for her.

"At least one of us should be decked out in finery. You are playing the part of the hostess. As I am still in mourning, I have been unable to wear anything nice."

"It is such a pity too because you have such nice features. You look so matronly in black. Once the year is up you shall have to dress in a different colour every day of the week. No, the month."

Sarah could only laugh at the exuberance with which Eloise began planning her wardrobe.

"If I am to be around the house, it would not matter what I wear."

"Nonsense, after this party everyone will be seeking your company. Perhaps you might even find someone that strikes your fancy."

She shook her head. "I am not rushing into matrimony so shortly after my last marriage."

"Well, you had better let Mrs. Rodes know that. She seems to have a very different opinion. She has told me she is to bring you a few suitors."

"What?" Sarah was truly shocked.

Eloise laughed behind her hands. "Well, you cannot escape the introductions now. It would be so rude."

"Maybe I shall take ill and not be at the party."

"No. You must. Think of what fun we shall have."

Sarah was unsure but played along.

Sarah had kept away for the remaining days of the week, so she had not heard about the visitor to the estate until her maid told her a Miss Glousen had arrived to be a companion to Mrs. Haverstock.

"I thought I was to be her companion."

"You will want to hear this, ma'am," her maid said, leaning forward to whisper. "Mr. Thorne sent her to the inn in the village. He said he did not have the rooms to house her and that there had been some misunderstanding."

Sarah gasped. "Did he really? And what did Mrs. Haverstock say?"

"I don't know the particulars, but harsh words passed between them."

"And tomorrow is the party..." Sarah said aloud without meaning to.

Her maid smiled, her eyebrows going up. "It shall not be dull, that is for sure."

Sarah nodded. She returned to her letters but was unable to focus much on them. Her mind was preoccupied with what had happened and whether there was a possibility Thorne would blame her for this latest development.

She flinched when she heard a knock at the front door. Peering out the window of the parlour, she saw the familiar figure of Mr. Thorne himself knocking at the door.

Sarah tried to school her features as she heard her maid answer the door. She adjusted her cap and smoothed out the pleats of her dress.

He was admitted to her room. Her maid left but did not close the door behind her.

She stood and bowed to him and he, remembering his manners, did the same.

"Lady Askew, did you have any idea that Miss Glousen was set to arrive here?"

Her eyebrows furrowed as she pretended to attempt to recall the name with no indication that she was aware of the fight that had taken place.

"I might have, but I did not recognize the name. Mrs. Haverstock showed me the list of invitations she wished to send out, and I approved it though I did not recognize most."

Her words seemed to have an effect on him. He considered her for a second and ceased his pacing.

"She...I would not have wished her to stay in my home. I apologize. I know I must have shocked you coming here like this," he said, straightening his jacket. "I have argued with my niece and she has taken to her bed. There is no reason for you to know that I dislike Miss Glousen," he said, taking a seat when she motioned him to one across from her.

"Would you like some tea?" she asked, interrupting whatever he was going to say next.

"No, thank you." He frowned and looked as though he was trying to collect his thoughts. "I think this garden party has got out of hand. I wasn't expecting to be surprised with Miss Glousen."

"Can I ask what your relationship is with her? Perhaps then I would understand the situation better. I cannot believe that Mrs. Haverstock would willingly invite someone you despised. She has a kind heart; I am sure she meant well."

Her words seemed to strike a chord with him. He let out a loud sigh as though he had been holding his breath in for quite some time.

"I reacted too rashly, even coming here as though to blame you. But, actually, I do have a favour to ask of you. Will you come and console Mrs. Haverstock? I worry for her, and I feel as though I have been a bad guardian to her. She refuses to speak to me. I may have reacted harshly."

Sarah nodded. "I would be happy to do so."

She could see how conflicted he was. As he watched the candles flickering, his expression seemed to soften.

"I was attached to Miss Glousen, but we had a falling out. She and Mrs. Haverstock were close friends back home, so I should not be surprised that she would wish to invite her. But she deliberately kept it from me and should have known I would not have wished to be reacquainted with her. It would be too uncomfortable..."

Sarah seemed to understand more and could greatly sympathize with him.

"She put you in a terrible position. It is understandable that you acted the way you did. I do not blame you in the slightest."

"At least someone doesn't. I do not deserve your kindness." His gaze now fixed on hers and she was forced to look away, embarrassed by the attention.

"She is a kind and trusting person. She is young and fanciful, but Mrs. Haverstock cannot be blamed for Miss Glousen's behaviour or her relationship with you."

"You are a fount of wisdom," he said, with a strained smile.

Sarah looked away from his gaze, as always finding it difficult to meet his eyes.

"Hardly, but I am still flattered."

"I see some misunderstandings have arisen on my part, and I am not yet too proud to admit I have made a few errors. Including giving Mrs. Haverstock the run of the house."

She watched as he ran a hand through his hair. In this light it looked like a deep chestnut brown. She remembered Maria calling him handsome and for the first time could agree with her, though she would never admit it to anyone.

"Shall I accompany you back to the house?" she asked.

"I have interrupted your work," he said, seeing the papers laid out on her writing desk. "And I must have given you a fright. I am a cad."

"Before you fall too deep into self-loathing, please do not worry." She gave him what she hoped was an eager smile. "I will be more than happy to help you with Mrs. Haverstock."

He waited for her outside while she threw on a cape

and tied a warmer cap to her head and shawl. She asked her maid to accompany her for propriety's sake. The sky was darkening overhead, and it would not do to have whispers about them. She would not trouble him to walk her back home either, but on the same token she did not wish to make the walk on her own.

"What happened to your roses?" he asked as she approached him.

She stood beside him, looking at the bare rose bushes.

"They were sacrificed to the garden party," she said, hoping she did not sound like she cared too much.

"What a pity..."

She looked up and saw that he was looking at her again.

"It was not an unwilling sacrifice, was it?"

Sarah shook her head. "I don't think even Mrs. Haverstock's enthusiasm for this party would make her forget her manners. I donated them willingly, but I will admit I was unprepared for how desolate my garden would look."

He replied with a thoughtful "Hmm," and they began walking back to the house. It took a good thirty minutes, but the fresh air did them both good.

Sarah could see the tension in his shoulders dissipating. As for Sarah, it was welcome exercise. She had taken to lounging about too much. Given that winter was fast approaching, this was not good. She would definitely be trapped indoors then.

Eloise Haverstock had still not left her room when

they arrived at the house. The tray of tea and toast was left abandoned by her door, growing cold.

Sarah squared her shoulders, picking up the tray with one hand and knocking with her free hand.

"Eloise, may I come in?"

There was silence for a moment, then she heard some mutters that she took to mean yes.

The curtains were drawn and only one candle was lit. The fire in the grate had died down to embers. It cast a gloomy atmosphere across the room. She set the tray down on a table and approached the figure on the bed.

"Eloise?"

"Yes?" came the half-choked sobs of what could have been a little child. Sarah frowned; it was a bit theatrical, but maybe it was because of the pregnancy.

"What has happened?"

"You must know since you are here," Eloise said with a tone of rudeness that Sarah did not appreciate.

"That is true, but I want to hear it from you. Besides, why have you locked yourself away in here? Let me call a maid to light a few more candles and stoke the fire. You should also eat something."

There was silence from Eloise, so Sarah pressed more.

"I promise you won't have to leave the room, but you wouldn't wish to appear at tomorrow's party with dark circles under your eyes. Let's have some tea and you can talk to me. Maybe you will feel better."

This made Eloise sit up. Her eyes were indeed puffy from crying—she had not been faking it.

"Very well," she said, giving Sarah a smile. "See how good I can be. You should tell my uncle."

Sarah laughed. "I am sure he would not treat you half so well if he did not know that. I'll just ring for the maid and bring you the tea."

She sat with her for the best part of an hour, listening to her huff and puff about how absurd it was that William had sent Miss Glousen away.

"I know he does not like her." At this she gave Sarah a knowing grin. "He was sweet on her at one time, but I don't think she felt the same. It doesn't matter; that was a long time ago. Or so I thought, but the way he reacted upon seeing her makes me doubt this now." She gave a chuckle and a sidelong glance at Sarah.

"Perhaps I might recruit you to help me get them together..." She snapped her fingers as though she had had a brilliant idea. "Yes, who better to soften him up!"

"I hardly think—"

"No, it would be perfect. He seems to respect you."

Sarah tried to contradict her but she merely rolled her eyes.

"It's not hard to see how he takes your advice. It is not like he has to." Eloise seemed keen on the idea. "You are his dear cousin."

Sarah nearly choked on a piece of toast and had to take a swig of tea. "I don't think I am that either."

Eloise tilted her head as though considering her. "What are you, then?"

"A nuisance."

This made her laugh. "Well, at the very least he sees

how serious you are and would take your advice seriously."

Sarah had to stop herself from contradicting her. Let Eloise make her little plans. She too knew the pang of missing a close friend.

"I don't ask much. Just ask him to let her stay for my sake. The past should be kept in the past. Don't you agree?"

Sarah nodded, but, pessimistic as she was, had to point out that sometimes this was not possible.

"He is very serious, but that is just his demeanour. He can hold grudges for a long time and is very sensitive. And maybe he will come to realize he still cares for Miss Glousen. Then you would truly have a friend to keep you company here forever."

Sarah felt like her head was whirling. Did Eloise really intend to play matchmaker with someone her uncle had thrown out of the house?

She bit the inside of her cheek. She could see how only someone in the depths of passion could react that way. After all, conventions of society would usually rule the heart...so maybe there was something there.

She was yet again caught in the middle, unsure what to do.

"I will help with what I can." She settled on not committing to anything.

"I knew you would help me. You are so good to me," Eloise said as she sipped her tea.

"Try to eat something too. You've been in a fit all evening."

To please her, Eloise nibbled at the toast and ate a bit of the tart laid out for her.

"Are you feeling better now? Shall I tell Mr. Thorne you have recovered you spirits?"

Eloise nodded.

"Then I will let you rest, and I shall see you tomorrow. It will be a splendid day and an even better party," Sarah said, giving her hand a squeeze.

She found William Thorne sitting in the parlour by the fire. He stood when she walked in.

"How is she?"

"Quite recovered. I think you may retire for the evening safely."

"I thought I would accompany you back," he said with a frown.

"There is no need to trouble yourself. My maid is with me; we shall be quite alright unless there are vagabonds hiding along the path."

His lips twitched in amusement.

"Please sit a while longer then. Tell me what she said. Is she very cross with me?"

Sarah took a seat opposite him, tying the shawl around her tightly. "I don't think she is the type of woman who can be cross for long. She is too happy a person."

He smiled at the compliment to his niece.

"I do think she just missed her friend. She alluded to there being something between you and Miss Glousen that happened a long time ago, but according to her that was dead and buried. I don't think there was any malicious intent on her part."

Sarah watched Thorne adjust his cravat. He was avoiding looking at her and seemed to be quite embarrassed by the unveiling of his past dealings. He regarded her once he had recovered himself.

"There is nothing much to say. As you said, it is in the past. I surprised myself by how I reacted upon seeing her. I shall have to apologize tomorrow."

"I think that would make Eloise very happy," Sarah said, standing up. She had nothing more to say, and it seemed as though Eloise was not wrong. Perhaps there was something there, and maybe it would not be such a bad thing to repair things between two people who might both still have feelings for each other.

CHAPTER SIX

The morning arrived too quickly for Sarah. She had trouble sleeping, thinking of Miss Glousen, Eloise, and Thorne. She was also nervous about how the event would go and hoped that no one would make a scene. William Thorne was too polite to try to do such a thing.

Her maid arrived and laid out one of her nicest black dresses. She would wear a dark bonnet to protect her from the sun, but she had added an arrangement of white flowers to make her seem less sombre. She knew, based on the decor and the clothing choices the other ladies would make, she would stand out like a sore thumb.

Knowing Eloise had wanted her to be there to greet guests and oversee the last-minute preparations, she headed towards the main house without eating much beforehand.

The house was in a flurry of activity. Servants were carrying the bouquets outside, as well as tables and lawn chairs.

It was already coming together quite splendidly.

The workers had also set up the tent that had caused such a fuss, but it did look grand. This was more of a festival than a mere garden party. She was eager to hear musicians play as well, since it had been such a long time.

Eloise appeared in a pale rose gown, hemmed with beautiful white lace. She had foregone a cap and was wearing her hair pinned up with red roses sticking out from it. The colours made her look flushed and youthful.

"I feel like a debutante again," she said, twirling for Sarah to see.

"It's a beautiful gown," Sarah complimented her, with a twinge of envy in her voice.

"And see the gloves you generously got for me." Eloise held out her hands. "They fit so well. I embroidered the little roses here."

"Very fine work," Sarah said admiringly.

"It is such a shame you are forced to wear such dowdy colours," Eloise commented, evidently unable to keep from saying something.

"I am used to it by now. But I am afraid I shall be miserably hot today."

"That's what the tent is for. See, I did it all for your comfort."

Sarah laughed. "Then I am very grateful."

William Thorne appeared downstairs too. He was dressed in a royal-blue suit. A colour that suited him very well with tan pants and black leather boots.

"Am I acceptable to you ladies?" he asked as he

descended the stairs before standing before them for inspection.

Sarah could see he had been freshly shaven too and thought she could catch the faint scent of cologne.

"What do you think, Sarah?" Eloise said, clutching her arm.

Sarah felt like her words were caught in her throat. "It is...I mean to say, you look put together."

Eloise let out a giggle. "You see, William, you shall have all the ladies blushing."

By now Sarah had indeed turned scarlet and was grateful for the bonnet helping to hide her face.

"I picked out his clothes myself. I wanted everything and everyone to look suitable."

Sarah nodded, still avoiding looking in his direction.

"I shall go and see that everything is going well. Our first guests should not be arriving for another hour or so," he said, looking at his pocket watch.

The two women were left to their own devices.

Eloise was too eager to sit down, and Sarah could not find a way to distract her other than playing at the pianoforte that had recently appeared in the drawing room.

"I had not noticed this last night," Sarah said.

"I suggested to my uncle that he might have one brought in. It is a pleasant past-time."

"But you do not enjoy playing..."

"No, but you do, and soon there might be many opportunities to dance."

"You cannot be thinking of dancing in your condition," Sarah said, looking pointedly at her growing belly.

Eloise waved a hand. "Then in the future, after I have given birth. I am sure there will be plenty of opportunities for music and dancing. Perhaps there shall even be a Mrs. William Thorne who would grace us with her music."

Sarah fell silent. She knew Eloise was thinking of one person in particular who might enjoy the pianoforte. Well, who was she to stand in the way? It would make her feel even more obsolete, though, and unwanted. If he did marry, she would leave and try to settle somewhere else, which was a shame since she had grown comfortable and accustomed to her little cottage.

She played another song, a jig to put her in a cheerful mood.

Thorne entered the room during the song. He brightened to see her playing and took a seat beside Eloise.

The song ended and the pair of them applauded.

"You play quite beautifully," he said.

"Thank you," Sarah said, fighting back the inclination to disagree with him.

"Yes, we need not have hired the musicians if I had known we had such a songbird among us."

"Please, I am hardly worthy of such praise. Nor do I find much joy in it as others do. But this is a fine instrument."

"I must show it to Miss Glousen," Eloise said, her eyes downcast, though she was peeking at Thorne to see how he might react.

Besides a pursing of the lips, he had nodded and said that he would be happy to allow her to have a tour of the whole estate.

Eloise took this to be a tiny victory and flashed Sarah a smile.

"We should wait in the garden for our guests. They should arrive any moment now."

Sarah watched him stand and go. He seemed under some strain, and she wished she could see him as relaxed as he had been before the topic of Miss Glousen was ever brought up.

"Thank you, Lady Askew," Eloise said quite formally. "We make a good team."

Sarah let herself be led away, her thoughts straying to William Thorne rather than the party.

Their guests, many of whom were neighbours, began arriving punctually. In such a quiet, small village there was not much to do, and a garden party was the height of excitement for everyone. Not to mention they wished to see what had become of the old house.

Sarah stood beside Eloise on the receiving line and was introduced to all as Lady Askew, the widow of Sir Ralph Askew, as she thanked them graciously for attending the gathering.

She found herself growing anxious as each introduction might bring her face to face with Miss Glousen.

At last, the famed guest arrived.

She was a vision of blue. A sheer layer of sky blue covered a pale blue underdress, the hem of which was decorated with little white flower buds, embroidered with white beads. The outfit was lavish and she looked stunning, and, as she greeted Mr. Thorne, Sarah could see that she was matching him in colour. This must have been a plan of Eloise's making, as she had picked his outfit.

She watched him as he greeted her.

He seemed overcome by her presence, but she could not hear what words passed between them.

He surprised Miss Glousen by inviting her to join them in the receiving line to greet the other guests. Sarah wondered at the slight envy she felt at this but was too distracted by greeting another neighbour. After everyone had arrived, they left to go greet their guests and mingle more.

Sarah kept to the outskirts of the party, unsure who to speak to and had seemed to be forgotten by both Eloise and William Thorne. She watched as Mr. Thorne offered Eloise his left arm and Miss Glousen his right as they strolled around speaking to people, ensuring everyone had what they wished for.

It was Mrs. Rodes, the parson's wife, who found her and pulled her off to the side.

"I have a few people I wish you to be introduced to in particular."

Sarah was surprised to find herself being led by the hand towards a group of older gentlemen.

They grinned as they saw her and bowed their heads.

"We've heard so much about you, Lady Askew," one said. A Mr. Browne if she remembered correctly.

"I have taken her under my wing," Mrs. Rodes said with a kindly smile.

Sarah could see she was missing a tooth, and wondered at her unkindness towards her.

She couldn't focus on the conversation; her attention kept being drawn to the lively conversation happening between Eloise and her group.

"Ah, the young have their fun," Mr. Browne said, following her gaze. "It's us old folk who are left to contemplate the world in quietude."

"Pardon?" She excused herself for being rude.

He smiled. "Mrs. Rodes tells me that you are originally from Essex, is that correct?"

"No, but close. My family is from Kent. We lived in Ashford."

"Ah, a shame. My mother was from Essex," he said, getting a little teary-eyed.

"Oh, I am sure it was a lovely place. Where does she live now?" Sarah suspected she must be deceased and, given the tears, perhaps recently.

"Oh, the saintly woman lives with me. You seem surprised, and yes, it is true she has lived to a great age. She looked after me very carefully; I was her only son, you see."

Sarah stood there listening to him go on about his mother for a quarter of an hour before being able to find some excuse to escape him.

"It was a pleasure speaking to you. I hope your mother's cough improves," she said, not waiting to hear his reply.

Perhaps it was rude of her, but she couldn't imagine wasting her whole day in his company.

She greeted a few people and went to get a plate of refreshments.

Mrs. Rodes came to find her.

"What did you think of him?" she said, a gleam in her eye.

"Mr. Browne? He seems like a nice gentleman."

"I knew you would think so. You seemed like a prudent lady. Not like others who are so flighty," she said, her eyes travelling over to the younger set.

Sarah frowned, starting to worry about what she was hinting at.

"Mr. Browne has two thousand a year. A very healthy income. He lives just a few miles away from here. I have told him you have a good income and inheritance that shall be yours upon your father's death."

"Pardon me!" Sarah nearly dropped her plate.

"What?" Mrs. Rodes seemed genuinely confused by her outburst.

"You cannot be suggesting that I...that we marry?"

She smiled at Sarah's question. "But of course I am, and if you don't like him, never fear—there are two other eligible gentlemen here for you to be introduced to."

Sarah took a step back from her as though she had burned her. "I thank you for your interest in my affairs, but you must know that I have no intention of marrying. As nice as I am sure these suitors are," she said with a shudder.

Mrs. Rodes now frowned. "Why? Are these men not

good enough for you, Lady Askew? Do you think we have not heard of what happened to your late husband? Perhaps you came here thinking we were a small village who did not receive the newspapers. But yes...the news travelled even as far as here of the most unfortunate event. I doubt you can afford to be particular, and don't think to pick off one of our young sons. They shall not fall prey to your wiles."

Sarah was genuinely taken aback now. How in the world had Mrs. Rodes come to this conclusion?

"That was not my intention in settling here."

She let out a little laugh, which grated on Sarah's nerves.

"You are in a good position, but surely you would consider settling down. These are good men from a good family. Perhaps they are not so young or handsome anymore, but they would be willing to take you. I have spoken to them myself."

"You have gone to a lot of trouble. But I am not a charity case. I am also not of a disposition to marry, especially not at the moment when I am still in mourning for my first husband." She said this with such an air of finality that Mrs. Rodes seemed affronted by her rudeness.

"Very well, if that is how you are," she said, following her gaze to where Mr. Thorne was speaking to Eloise and Miss Glousen as well as a few other people. "I see that you might have your sights set higher, but no one wants ruined goods. Pardon the expression. One day you will see how generous I was in even considering speaking for you. You had seemed like a good, serious sort of woman who had misfortune befall her, but now I am not so sure."

Sarah was thoroughly irritated but also embarrassed. She had not been looking at Mr. Thorne in that way. She had merely been wishing they would come to rescue her.

A tap on her shoulder made her turn around.

"Pardon me, Lady Askew, I believe you dropped this," a handsome man said; in his hand was a purse.

Sarah took a moment to recover. "Thank you...Mr. Featherston?"

He nodded. "A pleasure to speak to you again."

Seeing she was going to be ignored, Mrs. Rodes glared at the interrupting Mr. Featherston and strode away from her. Much to Sarah's relief.

After she was well out of earshot, Sarah thanked him.

"You seemed in need of rescuing," he said with a grin.

"Did I indeed?" Sarah laughed. "I must seem like a very sad person. Always pulled from one side to another. Always in need of rescuing."

"Nonsense," he said, giving her an appraising look. "You seemed to have been handling yourself quite well, but it would not do to completely alienate the parson's wife. She does have some influence in the neighbourhood."

Sarah nodded. "Then I must thank you for saving me from nearly making a grave error."

"You will have to agree to take a walk with me then," he said.

She blushed, finding this quite forward of him but

was unable to think of a reason to say no. She found herself drawn to this eccentric personality.

They walked about, him leading her around the perimeter of the party.

"Many changes have been made to Oakham since I was last here," he said.

She looked at him in surprise but then realized that as a local he must have been associated with the family here.

"How did you know the family?"

"I was acquainted with their daughter before she died," he said with some emotion, but then seeing her face fall, rushed to reassure her. "It was an accident that happened over four years ago now. She was a beautiful soul, so full of life and played the piano so beautifully. After her death, her mother kept planting roses all over the estate and moved into the cottage, unable to stand being near the house."

"I was not aware of this at all," Sarah said, gulping. The estate suddenly seemed so haunted by tragedy. "It explains a lot."

"Yes, after Mr. Wesley passed away his son sold the estate and moved with the mother far away from here."

"Now this place seems cursed, considering what happened to Sir Ralph," Sarah said as a chill travelled down her spine.

He stopped. "I have distressed you; I am terribly sorry."

She tried to calm herself.

"No. Thank you for telling me. No one has ever said

anything to me about it. Well, to be honest, I have not spoken to many people outside my own household."

He seemed to understand, though his pale blue eyes showed remorse. "I now feel indebted to you. I cannot believe I have brought such sadness upon you."

Despite herself, she found she was smiling. Trying to reassure this handsome young man that all was well.

"Mr. Featherston, after the year I have had, I don't think anything can shock me anymore."

"What? Not even a drove of suitors like Mr. Browne?"

They both laughed at his joke.

"I am afraid that came as a surprise to me," she found herself admitting.

A group of musicians had begun playing a tune.

Mr. Featherston looked towards the dance floor eagerly, then to her, an unasked question in his eyes.

"I dare not, Mr. Featherston. But I do thank you for the compliment of considering me," she said, feeling a heat rise from her collarbone to her neck.

"Then we must keep walking and speak of happier things," he said, offering her his arm.

Sarah hesitated but a moment before taking it. "How long have you lived here?"

"My whole life. I always dreamed of living somewhere else, but my fate has kept me tied to home."

"Even for your schooling?" She couldn't help but ask.

He nodded. "My father has tutors brought in for me. He did not want me corrupted."

She laughed. "Did he succeed?"

He grinned. "I am afraid I can never be reformed of my terrible habits."

"Which are?" She surprised herself with her flirtatious tone.

"Well, let me see...I enjoy playing cards too much, I have an incurable vanity, I like horses, I am too headstrong..." His voice trailed off as someone called to them.

Sarah looked up and saw that it was Eloise waving them over.

"Come along, Mr. Featherston, you can continue telling me of your faults another time." She led him towards her friend.

He greeted Eloise with a bow, placing a kiss on her gloved hand.

"You are as beautiful as any rose in this garden."

She blushed a pretty red.

"Who is this dashing man you found, Sarah?" she said with a grin.

"Mr. Featherston. He is a local from what I can gather."

"Ah, I thought he might be a travelling cad," Eloise said.

He laughed. "Have no fear of me. I am an incorrigible bachelor. The bane of my mother and father."

"I cannot imagine you being anything of the sort. I am sure you have a line of young ladies chasing after you," Eloise said. "And if not, then I could introduce you to a few."

Sarah snorted, unable to keep her amusement to herself and had to excuse herself. It was true that many eyes at the party followed him. He was tall, blonde, blue-eyed, and well-proportioned. She didn't know much about his family situation, but she supposed that it didn't matter so much when he had all these other attributes.

"And why are you not dancing, Mrs. Haverstock?" he said graciously.

"I am in the family way," Eloise said, a bit embarrassed.

"One would never have guessed."

"I think you may add 'flirt' to the list of faults you possess," Sarah said, in a joking manner.

He threw back his head, laughing, and drawing all eyes to him.

"You correct me, Lady Askew, and rightfully so. Shall you be the one to try to reform me?" he leaned in to whisper in her ear.

Sarah had to cough to hide the shiver of delight that coursed through her.

"You tease me, sir. But no, it will not be me that reforms you. I am too occupied with this house," she said, proud that she was able to keep her composure. Where was Maria to witness this?

Eloise watched their exchange with great amusement. Before anything further could be said, Mr. Thorne reappeared from the dance floor with Miss Glousen on his arm.

Sarah frowned at seeing them entwined as any two lovers. One would hardly believe that Mr. Thorne had thrown her out of the house just the night before.

He seemed to be both surprised and irritated by the presence of Mr. Featherston.

"Was it not splendid to dance?" Eloise asked. "It was wonderful to watch the two of you."

Mr. Thorne just grunted. "Your attention seemed diverted, so I am not sure how you could have known."

Eloise rolled her eyes and smiled at her friend.

"Please, introduce me to this handsome young man," Miss Glousen said. Her voice had a crystal-clear quality to it. Sarah wouldn't be surprised if it turned out she was musically inclined.

"This is Mr. Featherston," she said, performing the introduction as the eldest.

He bowed in response, but Sarah noticed that he did not kiss her hand. Should she feel that she was given some special attention? She found it unlikely that he would prefer her over the fashionable Miss Glousen, but stranger things had happened. Perhaps, as one of the hostesses of the party, he was paying her the compliment.

Sarah was eager to disappear from the group, feeling out of place in her black, a constant reminder that she was no longer playing the same game the others were.

She watched William Thorne whose gaze seemed to keep travelling unbidden to Miss Glousen. Could it be possible there was some true feeling there? Sarah wondered why Miss Glousen had refused him to begin with. But she wasn't the type of person to pry.

She tried to retreat to make the rounds around their guests and see if anyone needed anything. It would soon be time to serve the cake, a large confectionery piece that seemed as fine as her wedding cake.

She would go and speak to the housekeeper, but then she found her attention caught by Mr. Featherston.

"We never finished our conversation, Lady Askew," he said, walking up to her.

"You were busy making new acquaintances," she said, the ghost of a smile on her lips. It pleased her to receive attention, especially from a young handsome man, but she wasn't a fool.

"Yes," he said, looking over his shoulder. "I have never met such agreeable people in the neighbourhood in a very long time."

"Is that so?" Her eyebrow raised. "I must revise my opinion of you. You are not very charitable."

He chuckled. "When you have lived here long enough, and I hope you shall, you will see that the society here is deplorable and that I am more than generous. Far more generous than they deserve. Maybe one day Bluehaven will attract a fresh set of people into the neighbourhood and we will not be trapped with the elderly, whose favourite topic of discussion is their rheumatism."

"You shock me," Sarah said, but she was in fact amused. Taking a glance around the party she could see that they were indeed the younger people here. Many had left Bluehaven to make their fortunes or had chosen to settle somewhere more fashionable.

"You should dance, Mr. Featherston," she said, attempting to lead him back to Mr. Thorne.

"Why would I, when the one I wish to dance with is unavailable?"

She was proud of how she managed to hide her feelings of pleasure and embarrassment and maintain a cool composure. She looked at him from underneath her lashes and found him gazing at her with an intensity she had only read about.

"Mr. Featherston, you had better take care, or I will truly think you are some mad man. You'd better ask Miss Glousen to dance, lest people talk. I shall have no more of your pestering. It is not kind of you to tease me in this way. We have barely known each other for more than two hours," she scolded him, albeit gently.

He put a hand to his heart. "You have wounded me, Lady Askew. I shall do as you ask, so I might gain some favour with you. I shall count the days until you are free to be led out on to the dance floor."

"Go, you cad. Go. I shall not hear of you waiting around for me," she said, pushing him towards the waiting company.

Sarah watched as he bowed to Miss Glousen again and asked if he might have the pleasure of the next dance. She accepted, all the while keeping her eyes on Mr. Thorne as though she wanted to gauge his reaction. His expression was unreadable; even Sarah tried to study it to pick out some sentiment or emotion that might have slipped through his mask. But nothing.

They took up their positions in the next set, and Sarah found herself standing beside Mr. Thorne, watching the pair.

"They make a handsome couple," she said, unable to stand the silence between them as Mrs. Haverstock had disappeared to fetch a plate of food.

"Pardon?"

Sarah watched as he blinked once, twice, as though trying to clear his head.

"Were you lost in thought, Mr. Thorne? I don't believe I have ever seen you this way before," she said with a grin.

The corner of his lips twitched in amusement. "And you know me very well by now? Have you made a study of me?"

"No, just observations. In the schoolroom I could never focus long enough to study much of anything."

"I find that hard to believe; you have a good head on your shoulders."

She tilted her head in acknowledgement of the compliment.

"I was young and foolish then. I had all sorts of fanciful imaginations and no time for studying history or geography. Now I find that I wish I had paid more attention."

Mr. Featherston caught her attention. Even as he danced with Miss Glousen his eyes seemed to be following her. This left Sarah feeling flattered and pleased. The little interaction between the two was not lost on Mr. Thorne.

"Have you an inclination to change your circum-stances?"

The question, so forward and spoken without any

attempt at finesse, shook her.

"Mr. Thorne?"

"You are a free woman entitled to do as you please now. But don't make a fool out of yourself." He said this with such stiffness that she was brought back to the early days of their acquaintance.

"Mr. Featherston is a respectable young man. He is just playing the suitor, but there is nothing I could offer him. Is it wrong to enjoy some frivolity?" she asked him, turning to face him. He had done likewise.

They were now face to face, inches apart. Sarah could feel his breath on her face and she had to step back.

"You have much to offer a man," he said, then his glance went over to the couples dancing. This would have sounded like a compliment had he not continued after a pause. "But I would be wary of him. You are a widow, as you keep reminding me yourself, but you have certainly not acted like one today."

The words stung more than she would care to admit.

"I will not be rebuked by you of all people. If you care so much about propriety then perhaps you would not have thrown Miss Glousen out of your house only to dance with her the next day," she said, unable to stop the words pouring out in anger.

Out of the corner of her eyes she could see that they were drawing attention to themselves.

She straightened up and tried to relax, stepping back.

"Please excuse me," she said, and left.

Sarah acted as normal as possible. Luckily, no one here knew her well enough to pick up on the tightness in her smile. She got pulled into a conversation with some other ladies. They wanted to bring her into a scheme to raise some money and provisions to help the poor people relying on the parish for food and clothing.

"Would you be interested in helping us?" Mrs. Greencroft said, as she took another biscuit from a passing tray.

"Oh yes, I'd love to help any way I can," Sarah said.

"Excellent. What the people in our parish need most is clothes for the winter, and food of course. Whatever you can spare."

Sarah nodded. "I am not greatly skilled with a pair of knitting needles, but I can make scarves and hats. As for food I shall send whatever I can from my own supplies. It pains me to think that good honest families would go hungry, especially at Christmas time."

Mrs. Greencroft nodded, looking to Mrs. Reed. "We had something ambitious planned this year for the Christmas season. You tell her, Mrs. Reed."

The small bent-over old lady seemed energized by the topic. "Well, we wanted the church hall to be emptied out and a soup kitchen of sorts to be set up where we could hand out food and serve these families a proper meal. Most were good honest working people until the recent...changes," she said with a frown. "My husband does not like me talking about such things, but at least we can help."

"That sounds excellent."

"The trouble is we haven't had the approval of the parson's wife."

"Why not ask him, then? Surely such a good act of Christian charity is worthy of the small sacrifice of giving up the church hall."

"Yes, we think so too, but we dare not go around her. She would make our life difficult," Mrs. Greencroft chimed in.

"I'll try speaking to her again. If we add more voices to the request, surely she could not deny us." Sarah was sure that if she could convince a few more people to join the cause then it would force Mrs. Rodes' hand. She didn't mind getting on her bad side. She was sure she was already there. What could such a woman do to her?

The dance must have ended, for she saw Mr. Featherston approaching with a slight spring in his step.

"Hello, Mrs. Greencroft, Mrs. Reed. The pair of you are as beautiful as ever," he said to them with a bow.

They giggled and swatted at his shoulder.

"You cannot tease such old ladies like this," Mrs. Reed said, though Sarah could see how it pleased her.

"Nonsense, I just did, and I will continue to do so," Mr. Featherston said, as though he was making a grand declaration. "What were you three discussing?"

The other two ladies remained tight-lipped, but Sarah had no qualms about sharing their plans.

"How we might help the poor. I have been invited to help as I can."

"A worthy use of your time," Mr. Featherston said.

"I thought so too," Sarah said with a smile, happy to see he approved.

"You commanded me to dance but you did not stay to watch," he said, admonishing her to her embarrassment.

"I wanted you to enjoy the party, not cater to a widow like me," Sarah said, though her own words were teasing.

Even the other two ladies giggled.

"We shall not keep you from enjoying yourselves," Mrs. Greencroft said. "I shall pay you a call on Tuesday if you are home; we can discuss it more then. A pleasure to meet you."

Sarah smiled. "I shall eagerly await your visit."

The two ladies left, and she watched them go, her heart light that she seemed to have a new purpose and something worthwhile to do with her time.

"You seem to make friends left and right despite your assurances to me that you are quite dull and shy," Mr. Featherston said.

She couldn't help but look away embarrassed. "I think you are teasing me and that is unfair."

"Then I apologize; it was not my intention to make you uncomfortable. Though the way you blush is awfully enticing."

"Mr. Featherston, please...someone might overhear you. I can hardly pretend to have the sort of charms that would make men fawn over me. There are other ladies here who would be more than pleased to hear such words from you."

He seemed castigated. "I shall have to promise to keep my compliments to myself then, if they make you feel so. As for the other ladies, I do not feel like bestowing my favour upon them."

"Now I have insulted you," Sarah said, hearing the hurt in his voice. She let out a heavy sigh. "Let's be friends, and you may stop flirting with me or you will slip from my high regard."

He seemed cheered by her words.

"Very well, I accept your terms," he said at last. "Tell me, do you ride?"

"Yes, but I do not currently keep a horse."

"Then we must rectify this..."

She gave him a pointed look and he held his hands up in surrender.

"You never let me finish, Lady Askew," he said with a grin. "I have a full stable. You must borrow a horse as it pleases you. Then I may show you the beautiful sights of Bluehaven."

That did sound pleasant. She couldn't deny it.

"Very well, I shall agree to it."

"Good, you shall have to start keeping a calendar and start booking people in to keep track of all of your appointments and visits."

Sarah laughed. "I shall be a proper lady of the manor indeed."

"And what of Mr. Thorne? Is he to be married? The way he glared at me when I led Miss Glousen off the dance floor made me quite sure I had done him some terrible wrong."

She looked over to them. Miss Glousen was talking to Eloise, laughing and chattering away, but Mr. Thorne, who had seemed to be a part of their party, was not looking at them but rather in her direction. Their eyes met and she was forced to look away.

"I could not say, but he does seem to have a history with her," she said.

"Perhaps, now that he has come into his inheritance, he can afford to think of marriage," Mr. Featherston speculated.

Her nod was slow, as she tried to decipher from his expression if he meant anything else. He was looking off into the distance, a sort of wistful expression, before looking back towards her and smiling.

"Excuse me, I was lost for a moment there," he said.

"On the contrary, but let us move away from a topic more suited to gossiping old housewives. Tell me more about yourself. Do you enjoy reading? How do you spend your time?"

They began strolling again among the party guests, stopping every once in a while for Sarah to accept the compliments of a neighbour or two.

"I go hunting when I can, but I hardly spend as much time as I would like reading. My family library is quite extensive, but I am never in it. I shall blame the drafts that keep me away."

Sarah couldn't help grinning. "I did not know young men such as yourselves had such weak constitutions."

"Oh, we do. We just usually don't share it."

"Then I am flattered you have decided to confide in me," she said.

The conversation from there flowed easily, leaving Sarah to wonder where the better part of an hour went.

The sky was no longer as bright, and their guests were beginning to head home. Overall, she felt the party was a great success, even if it was just because for the first time in a long time she had enjoyed being out in company and meeting new people. The earlier incident with Mrs. Rodes was forgotten, and if Mr. Browne still had any inclination for pursuing her, he had not approached her again.

She bade farewell to Mr. Featherston, having been given the promise of his calling on her again. She would have to keep an agenda soon for all her appointments. Including the ones with Mrs. Greencroft and Mrs. Reed. Her days would soon be filled with excitement and work. More than ever she was happy to have made the decision to come settle here.

She would write as much to Maria, whose latest letters mentioned that she was worried about her sanity. Sarah also wrote an especially long letter to Louisa, who had been missing her company lately. Their mother had been forcing her to attend all sorts of lessons she had no interest in, from dance to music. Sarah was sympathetic to her plight.

Soon it was just the four of them left, Mr. Thorne, Eloise, Miss Glousen, and herself.

The other ladies had gone inside to have a rest, but she and Mr. Thorne stayed to oversee the staff taking down the decorations. She had wanted to walk home herself but didn't want him to think she was shirking her duties.

Sarah directed that the flowers should be brought

inside and put in vases. There was no point in wasting them just for one party. The leftover food should be collected and sent over to the parish church to be doled out to the unfortunate. This was something she had forgotten to consider doing sooner. As a general principle she hated waste and was happy to know there was something she could do to help those less fortunate.

Mr. Thorne had still not said a word to her. She was certain at times she could feel his eyes burning holes in the back of her head. It created a very tense atmosphere outside. She wasn't sure if others could feel it, but she couldn't shake the feeling. By the time the tent was being taken down, she was ready to run away.

Uncharacteristically for her she did not.

She'd had a nice day, and she wasn't about to let him ruin it.

She turned to face him as the last of the furniture was taken in, a wide smile on her face.

"Well, I would say that was a very successful afternoon," she said, inviting him to challenge her.

He had simply nodded and turned on his heel to go inside.

She frowned, looking after him and almost called out to him, but let him go.

This wasn't a battle she would win, not with someone so determined to be cross. She wasn't even sure over what.

CHAPTER SEVEN

With a four-day respite Sarah put her little cottage in order, eagerly awaiting the visitors she would be receiving. She made sure that the cook would order extra fruit and sugar to have on hand for little finger foods she might serve them.

Eloise had paid her a brief visit, accompanied by Miss Glousen, on the day after the party.

"How did you enjoy your little garden luncheon?" she asked, trying to appear bright and cheerful.

"It was very sweet. I shall hope to be invited more often to such events." The response was cool and perfectly said.

Sarah got the feeling that Miss Glousen prided herself on being very well put together.

She offered them some tea, not noticing how downcast Eloise seemed.

"So what are your plans?"

"Well, I had hoped to stay a few days, but I am afraid

141

business shall take me back to London shortly," Miss Glousen said.

This made Eloise stir in her seat; she had been lost in thought.

"I am still sure William might be persuaded," she said, looking from her friend and back to Sarah as though an idea had struck her.

Sarah put her hands up to stop her in her tracks. "I will wish you all the luck in the world, but I am afraid that I cannot intercede with your uncle. He is not on speaking terms with me at the moment."

The two women looked at her with sly expressions.

"What?"

Eloise grinned. "It might have something to do with the favour you showed a certain someone."

"I don't know what you mean." Sarah twirled the tea in her cup with a spoon, adding another lump of sugar.

"We are referring to Mr. Featherston," Miss Glousen chimed in, helpful as ever.

Sarah's mouth formed an "o" shape and she looked down at her cup, embarrassed. "I hate how people jump to conclusions. He is pleasant company to have around."

"Yes, and it helps that he is handsome," Eloise said with a laugh.

Even Miss Glousen chuckled, acknowledging this as fact.

"Well, it shouldn't matter then to Mr. Thorne. Unless he is worried that I am out husband-hunting. I would never do anything to bring scandal upon myself or family or relations. He need not be concerned. I already told him that I am not inclined to remarry. But I suppose he and every other person believe I do not know my own heart."

The two women across from her were grinning from ear to ear.

"You know very little about men," Miss Glousen commented, picking up her teacup and taking the most delicate of sips.

Sarah frowned, waiting for some explanation as Eloise nudged her friend with her foot. It was then that Miss Glousen glanced at her through hooded eyes.

"Men are jealous creatures. If they see something someone else has that they don't...well, they want it."

"You seem very knowledgeable," Sarah said through pursed lips. She did not care for the direction this conversation was going in. She glanced at Eloise to see what she was making all of this, but she seemed unfazed. This was apparently nothing new or shocking to her.

The chink of china as Miss Glousen set down her cup made Sarah turn her attention back to this stranger.

"I have not the luxury you possess of being a wealthy widow at such a young age, but I have had my fair share of acquaintances. Unfortunately, I do not have the sort of dowry that would attract a suitable husband. Most women don't. We must rely on our other skills..." She paused, a knowing smile spreading over her face as she regarded Eloise. "You know, our smiles, our conversation, and quick wit. To be always superior in every way to everyone else. You become enthralling," she said, each word rolling off her tongue as smooth as silk. "That is the way for us in the world. You are lucky. But now you've become quite the catch yourself, and I would watch out if I were you—more dangerous fortune hunters than the likes of Mr. Featherston will appear at your door. Are you prepared?"

Sarah's heart was beating faster as she tried to remain composed. Such language, and in her own home. Threats and intrigue all rolled into one. She regarded Miss Glousen as though suddenly two pieces of the puzzle finally fit together.

"Tell me, how have you found the house? And Mr. Thorne? I know from him myself that he was not pleased to see you upon your arrival. Have you made headway in that direction? Or is he just as unattainable as before?"

Eloise looked shocked, her mouth gaping open, but Miss Glousen threw back her head and laughed, the ostrich feather in her hair swaying dangerously close to falling out.

"It was I who turned down his proposal the first time. I had my sights set higher." Miss Glousen said this with such perfect indifference that Sarah was blown away. How could someone be so heartless? Or appear to be so?

"And what business do you have with me?" she said into the silence of the room.

"Me? Nothing. I have come to see how you fare here. You have quite the cosy arrangement. It could have been me in your shoes, had things gone differently. Luckily, you had the dowry that trumped any of my attractions. So I suppose I came to ask for your help, but I find that I am playing the part of the teacher to you," Miss Glousen said. There was an air of gravity as she spoke and a certain gleam in her eye.

Sarah realized she was getting a lot of satisfaction from this.

"Are you waiting for me to cry out in shock or amazement?" Sarah looked at her with pity; this was something Miss Glousen wasn't expecting.

"Vicky, we should go," Eloise said, in a quiet voice, but her supposed friend shook her off. She was staring daggers at Sarah, but Sarah wasn't done yet.

"Would you like to see a detailed list of my accounts so you may know more accurately the value of the fortune you missed out on? Are you so angry with yourself for ruining your chance with Mr. Thorne? Are you imagining what you could have had if you had only said yes to him at the time? It must really be tearing you up inside."

Miss Glousen was on her feet ready for a brawl. She was breathing heavily, and Sarah was quite certain she might indeed be inclined to throw a blow her way.

Luckily for all of them they were interrupted by her maid entering the room.

"Shall I stoke the fire, Lady Askew? Or bring out some cake?"

"No, thank you," Sarah said, her eyes never leaving Miss Glousen, who was trying to gather herself. She watched the transformation of the angry spitfire behind the veil of pallid beauty that she liked to present to the world.

"We shall go now. Thank you so much for your time.

I hope you enjoy your little cottage for a long time to come," Miss Glousen said, with a toothy smile that made Sarah think of a cat baring its teeth.

"Eloise, are you well?" Sarah said, turning to the pregnant woman she had regarded as a friend these last few weeks.

Eloise looked pale, and a hand was pressed to her head.

"I feel light-headed," she admitted at last.

Sarah frowned and walked over to examine her more closely. Despite the fact she had brought this viper into Oakham, she couldn't ignore her. Nor would she blame her for her friend's words. Though it was clear that Eloise kept bad company.

"I don't feel comfortable letting you walk back to the house. You must rest here while I send a note to your uncle; he shall know what to do." Sarah stood and looked at Miss Glousen who seemed to be irritated by the delay in their departure.

"Will you carry the note?"

The way her lips pursed made her think that no, she had no inclination to do so, but the situation would cast such an unfavourable light on her that she was forced to agree.

"Of course, anything for a dear friend," she said at last, taking a seat next to Eloise again, placing what seemed like a comforting hand on her elbow.

Sarah wasted no more time and walked over to her writing desk and scrawled out a messy note and handed it to her.

Miss Glousen said something under her breath to Eloise that she could not hear.

Sarah watched Eloise nod, and Miss Glousen left the room.

Once she was gone Sarah let out a breath.

"Eloise, you had best lie down. Stretch your legs out on the couch," Sarah said, ringing the bell for the maid.

"Please prepare some chamomile tea for Mrs. Haverstock; she is unwell. And bring me a basin with water and a washcloth, if you please."

Sarah pulled up a chair beside Eloise and held her hand.

"Does something in particular hurt you?"

Eloise shook her head. "No, but I-I hate to be around people having arguments."

Sarah bit her lip to keep from laughing. "That was nothing. Though I can't say I am not surprised at Miss Glousen for having such nerve."

"She means well. She has had awfully bad luck. She's truly a nice person; she just doesn't often show it."

Sarah busied herself arranging the cushions so Eloise could be more comfortable, so she wouldn't have to contradict her. It was a test of her patience that she hadn't thrown Miss Glousen out earlier.

"You must rest," she said. "Your uncle will have my head if anything happens to you under my roof."

Eloise managed a strained smile. "I fear he may, regardless. I have displeased him greatly."

"He will forgive you anything. My mother always said that is the privilege of a pregnant woman," Sarah said, in a light tone. "Now hush, and don't worry, just rest."

They did not have to wait long for Mr. Thorne to appear. He had ridden down on his bay mare as fast as he could.

He hadn't even bothered knocking on the door of the cottage but strode right in. Sarah, who had seen this from the window of her parlour, still jumped to her feet in surprise when he suddenly entered the room.

"What has happened?"

"She began feeling unwell and dizzy. I thought it would be best not to move her," Sarah said, a hand on Eloise's shoulder. "She seems a bit better now. I gave her some tea, and sponged her forehead with cool water. I did not know what else to do."

"I have called for the doctor; I hope he shall make haste." Mr. Thorne walked over to his niece, concerned only for her well-being. It was sweet to see such care and devotion.

Eloise tried to assure him that she was recovering.

"You did not eat well enough at breakfast. I shall have to keep a closer eye on you," he said as though scolding a child.

"Apologies," Eloise said.

Her voice sounded far away again. Almost weak. It appeared to both of them that she was feeling faint again and tired.

"Rest now," he said, placing a kiss on her forehead.

As he turned back to her, Sarah could see how deep his concern really was.

"The doctor will come soon," he said, but it sounded more like he wanted to reassure himself.

"Do you think we should move her upstairs to one of the bedrooms where she might be more comfortable?" Sarah asked. "I did not know what to do and that's why I called for you."

He considered this but shook his head. "It would be better to keep her here. Hopefully we can find a way to get a carriage down here to carry her to the house."

"She can also stay here as long as necessary. I am capable of looking after her," Sarah said. "I mean if the doctor thinks she should not be disturbed."

He straightened and bowed his head.

"I am grateful for your offer."

"I am too," came Eloise's weak voice. "But it would be better for me if you stopped talking about me like I was dead or dying."

Sarah fought the urge to apologize.

"Shall I read to you? Or play you some music?"

"No, it is fine." Eloise closed her eyes again.

Sarah shared a look with Mr. Thorne. They both took seats around the ailing woman. With some amusement Sarah watched him debate which seat to take. He wanted to remain as far from her as possible and yet be near at hand.

At length the doctor appeared at the door, in his black coat. He was a middle-aged man with a serious countenance, but he was kind and listened attentively to both Sarah and Eloise as he asked them a series of questions. He felt her pulse and listened to her heartbeat, examining her as best he could.

"As far as I can tell, you need rest and to stay away from anything that might excite you. You are in a precarious situation, Mrs. Haverstock. You seem to have escaped any serious consequences, but I would take care. You should keep yourself calm. So no parties or long journeys." He turned to Mr. Thorne to further assure him that all was well.

"If there's anything else, you should call for me," he said as he bade them good night.

Mr. Thorne went to settle the bill with him and then returned to the room.

"May she sleep here tonight? And tomorrow, if she is better, I will move her back to the main house," he said to Sarah.

"Of course. You do not need to ask me. I would gladly do it," she said as she looked over at Eloise.

When she looked up again, she could see him regarding her with all the seriousness of a barrister.

"May I speak to you outside?" he asked at last.

"Certainly." She followed him out the door, instructing her maid to sit with Eloise until she returned.

Sarah shivered as the evening air pierced through her thin dress despite her shawl. She had not changed out of her evening gown.

Thorne was shifting from one foot to another, looking more uncertain by the second from the way his eyes seemed unable to settle on anything in particular.

"I need to know what happened when she took ill?"

Sarah tightened the shawl around herself.

"Lady Askew..."

She couldn't take the pressure of lying or of fabricating a story. Sarah settled on telling him most of the truth.

"The three of us were having tea and the discussion grew heated. I should have kept my temper, and I would not have even continued the conversation had I known how it would affect Mrs. Haverstock. She has grown dear to me these last few weeks. That is all I can say on the matter," she said.

Thorne looked as though he wanted to say more, but he must have seen how resolute she was not to divulge more information. He ran a hand through his hair, something she had seen him do often, whenever he was frustrated.

"Thank you, Lady Askew," he said. "I shall know what to do. But first I'll go and send Eloise some essentials from the house." William Thorne began walking up the path towards the main house.

Sarah bit her lip.

"Wait, one moment," she called out, at last having gathered her courage. "Mr. Thorne, it is no one's fault. Some words were said in anger, but Eloise was not involved in this. If anything, I am to blame."

He turned his head to look at her. "And Miss Glousen? Is she not to blame as well?"

"She is Eloise's dear friend...I know how much such a relationship can mean to someone," she said, trying to explain as best she could. Did Sarah approve of Miss

Glousen? No. But she could sympathize with Eloise. Like herself and Maria, Eloise and Miss Glousen had known each other for several years.

He turned his back to her.

She watched him go, unsure of what he would do next. Unwilling to go chasing after him or leave Eloise, she turned back to the house and the warmth of the fire.

Eloise was in better spirits by the next morning. She had slept past ten in the morning.

Sarah was surprised to see both Mr. Thorne and Miss Glousen appear at her door. Miss Glousen looked chastened but, in a way, triumphant.

Sarah couldn't help but wonder what had occurred.

"Come in. Eloise is getting dressed," she said as they entered.

"Good, I am glad to hear she is in better spirits. I have brought Miss Glousen to help me. We have agreed she will stay on to nurse her friend and look after her."

Sarah opened her mouth but shut it again quickly. She was in no position to protest or anything to the contrary.

"I am sure Eloise will be happy to hear the news."

Miss Glousen smiled, putting a hand over her heart. "It is my greatest desire to see my friend on the mend. I am sure under my care she will recover splendidly."

"Yes, and thus we shall not have to trouble you, Lady

Askew. Though I am grateful for the services you provid-ed," Mr. Thorne added.

Sarah looked from one to the other and, with a shrug, nodded. Why did she not like the sound of that? But what could she say that would not upset everyone, including Eloise? Mr. Thorne seemed to have a good head on his shoulders. It would be up to him to look out for himself.

Miss Glousen had warned her of fortune hunters and people waiting to take advantage of others. She could not protect everyone nor was it her job. It hurt her perhaps, that he had not thought to ask for more of her assistance, but she realized this was for the best. She shouldn't be spending her time on this. She should be looking out for her own interests too. Too often she was constantly trying to overstretch and exert herself on behalf of others. Perhaps it was for the best to take a step back from that.

Eloise made an appearance, holding on to her maid's arm for support.

She cheered considerably to see Miss Glousen and Mr. Thorne together.

"They have come to take you home," Sarah said. "They shall do a much better job than me at looking after you."

"Nonsense, you have been a superior companion," Eloise said.

Miss Glousen stepped forward to take her arm. "We are all very grateful to you for your kindness."

Sarah gave her a strained smile. If she was going to act as though nothing had happened, then she too could put it all in the past. It was healthier to not dwell on such matters.

"I shall come and pay you a visit tomorrow to see how you do. Or perhaps, Mr. Thorne, you can send me a note to let me know how she is faring? If it is not too much trouble," Sarah said, turning to him.

"It would be no trouble."

She watched them leave, Eloise supported between the pair of them as her maid and two manservants followed behind with a trunk of her things that had been sent over.

The house was quiet at last. Sarah, exhausted and emotionally drained, from a night of watching at Eloise's bedside, took to her bed for a midday siesta.

The following day, after breaking her fast and changing out of her day dress, she was pleasantly surprised to find Mr. Featherston appear at her door, a bouquet of wild-flowers in his hand.

"Good day," she said to him, accepting the gift. "These are lovely."

"I am glad you like them. They weren't so well received at the main house," he said, accepting the seat she offered him.

"Oh?"

He had a mischievous grin on his face. "I stopped by to pay my respects and give them a note from my parents to thank them for their hospitality. But I am afraid that

Miss Glousen wasn't thrilled to see my gift. I suppose she prefers flowers from the hothouse."

Sarah did not wish to disillusion him.

"Well, I am glad it did not dissuade you from visiting me. How are you?"

She watched as he leaned back in his seat, well at ease already in her company and in the house.

"I have been bored out of my mind, but that is nothing new," he said. "I was waiting eagerly for Tuesday to come around."

Sarah supposed this was her cue to giggle and blush, but she did neither of those things.

"Can I offer you some refreshment?"

"No, but if I may take you on a walk around the grounds, that would be enjoyable."

She liked the sound of that and instructed her maid to come along with them. If Mr. Featherston was displeased by this, he did not let himself show it, but she wasn't a fool to invite talk. His company was pleasant, but she could not trust his character. They had just been introduced, and despite Miss Glousen's insinuations that she wasn't worldly, she knew enough to know to protect herself.

They walked all the way to the end of the road, giving the house a wide berth. He took her down an overgrown path that led them to the ruins of a pavilion.

"This is a very old building. The previous owners used to use it for their own garden parties. It was all the rage to copy buildings from antiquity."

Sarah was mesmerized by the crumbling ruins. She

imagined this is what the temples must look like in Greece now.

"I had not known about this." She moved closer and was about to take a step to go up on the platform, but a hand stopped her.

"Best not to," Mr. Featherston said with a smile. "Wouldn't want you getting hurt. Perhaps Mr. Thorne will see to it that this place is repaired."

She nodded, her hand reaching out to touch a pillar. Moss had grown on the white stone and a vine was clawing its way up.

"With so many projects at the house I am not surprised this has been neglected. It looks like something out of a fairy tale."

"I knew you would appreciate it," he said. He walked around, inspecting it for something.

"What are you looking for?"

"There's something..." He was moving some foliage around. "Ah, here it is." He had ripped some of the vines away. "Here is the inscription."

She came around to see.

It was a poem and read:

She – as sweet as the summer sun,
Deigned to meet me in a glen,
My heart ablaze reached out to her,
Yet her words whispered in my ear cut deep,
Nevermore – nevermore shall I ever be yours,
My love

"That's beautiful," she said.

"Thank you." He looked up, grinning. "I wrote it."

"You are a man of many surprises," Sarah couldn't help but say. It was rare for her to come across a man with such an open, courteous countenance. It was a pleasant surprise and welcome change.

"Ah, it was nothing. A few scribblings, but he liked it enough to have it inscribed. They called this the lovers' pavilion; however, nothing grander than a party happened in this grove."

Sarah took a step away from him, realizing she had gotten too close. This talk of love made her flustered.

"Shall we head back to the house?"

"Yes." Mr. Featherston straightened up. "Will you do me the honour of offering me a cup of tea?"

She smiled at his daring but nodded. "You would make a good tour guide for the region. You seem to know so much and all these little secrets. It is a shame more do not know of them."

"Most do not care, Lady Askew. They are content to sit confined in their houses. The spark of adventure was doused a long time ago for the people who remain here."

"You should consider taking up a post overseas then. I see that you would enjoy it a lot," Sarah said, accepting the offer of his hand as they came upon uneven ground.

"I have thought of it. Maybe a job with the East India Trading company or the army—"

"No, not the army," she said, interrupting him. "That would be to put you foolishly in harm's way."

"You mean I should not defend my country? It is a

noble cause to die for one's nation. People have died for less."

Sarah shook her head. "If I would have anything to say about it, we would all be at peace. I cannot countenance so much senseless death."

He raised an eyebrow at her passionate words, and she had to apologize.

"My heart breaks every time I read in the papers of a father, uncle, or brother dying in this war. I wish it were not the case."

"Life is full of risks."

The way he said that made Sarah look at him more closely. There was such a heaviness in spirit about him now. Some great weight bearing down on him. He was not quite the easy-going philanderer that he liked to present himself as.

They reached the cottage, and they sat outside picking at food, not really talking about anything in particular. The leaves were starting to turn, a sure sign that winter was on its way. How many more days would there be until it would be too cold to venture outdoors for long?

Finally, he excused himself, and she bade him farewell.

"I shall come and visit you again, if you will have me, and you must call upon my family if you ever grow bored of your own surroundings," he said from atop his horse.

Sarah nodded and waved him off.

She returned inside to see to the correspondence she had been neglecting for quite some time. She would have to remember to ask her parents for details about when she should journey to see them and how long she should plan on staying for. She was at their disposal.

"You have a very comfortable room here," Mrs. Reed said, once she had finished conducting a tour of it, occasionally lifting a bauble to inspect it more closely.

"Thank you," Sarah said with sincerity. "When you are better, I should like to give you a tour of the grounds as well."

Mrs. Reed nodded. She was currently walking with a cane; a bad fall had left her with a twisted ankle. Sarah had been surprised she had still come, but she assured her she was not the sort to sit around idly in bed.

"I am afraid the doctor thinks I am his worst patient," she said as though confessing a dreadful secret. "I never take my bedrest, and I never take the medicines he prescribes for me. I am hopeless, Lady Askew."

Sarah had to hide a smile, not wishing to appear impolite.

The trio took their seats and got down to business. They laid out the work, and they did what they needed and provided her with a list of families in need in the neighbourhood.

"There are so very many people on this list," Sarah said, a pang of guilt striking her.

"Yes," Mrs. Greencroft said, sharing a look with Mrs. Reed. "A tragedy that the common land was taken away. Many people used to work on the farms as well; the women too would winnow the chaff from the wheat. Now there's less work to go around. I am all for advancement, but it is a pity more cannot be done for them."

Sarah nodded. "Well, I am happy to roll up my sleeves and get to work."

"That's the spirit, my dear," Mrs. Greencroft said, patting her knee. "Always happy to see some of you young folk still care about the welfare of others. So many are caught up in their little worries and they don't pay attention to those less fortunate around them."

"At least we shall have you to correct us and set us on the right track," Sarah said.

They smiled at her kind words.

She promised them that she would come to their weekly meetings and figure out what she could donate and give.

"I would be more than happy to keep a lookout for work and jobs that many of these people might do, even if it is in another county. A fund could be set up to assist them to move if it is necessary."

"That's a very good idea. We cannot wait to hear the details."

Just as they stood up to leave, Sarah heard a knock at the door.

"I wonder who that could be," she said, trying to peek out the window, but her vision was obscured.

Not long after, her maid knocked on the door to announce none other than Mr. Thorne, hat in his hand.

He seemed to be surprised that she had company and apologized.

"I am sorry to have disturbed you," he said after all formal greetings were concluded.

"Nonsense, young man," Mrs. Greencroft said. "We were just on our way out. Weren't we, Abigale?"

Mrs. Reed nodded. "Yes, please don't let us keep you. Have a good day, Lady Askew, Mr. Thorne."

Sarah bowed to them, finding them more endearing than ever.

She escorted them to the door and bade them farewell.

"They are very nice and so kind to have taken me under their wing," Sarah said, turning back to Mr. Thorne.

"Yes, I am sure they are. Be careful they don't take the carpet from under you."

"What do you mean?"

"Charity is admirable work, but you wouldn't wish to go bankrupt while helping the less fortunate."

"I am not that hopeless with finances. Never fear," she said, as she began tidying up the papers on the table.

"How are you? How is Eloise?" she said at last, guessing why he had come to see her.

"She is well."

"Good..." She looked at him quizzically.

"Well, good day. I shall not keep you." He was halfway out the door when Sarah called out to him.

"Surely that was not the only reason you came all this way?" She was perplexed by his strange behaviour.

When he turned around, she thought she could see the hint of a blush on his cheeks.

"No, I was walking this way and I thought I'd stop in to check on you."

"That is very kind of you," she said, placing the papers on her writing desk to be sorted later. But Sarah was still not buying it; his behaviour was all too suspicious. He was standing there in the doorway, one foot out into the hallway, one still in her parlour.

He must have guessed her thoughts.

"I was curious who was visiting. You've been receiving a lot of visitors lately, and I was concerned."

Sarah laughed. "Why would you be concerned?"

He could not meet her eyes.

"No reason. I was merely thinking that you, as a widow on your own, are so far away from any help, and you are so trusting you would open your door to anyone."

Including you? she thought, but she did not say this out loud.

"I have my household, so I am hardly alone." She found his concern peculiar.

"Yes."

She found herself at a loss for words. What was she supposed to say?

"Would you like to join me for lunch?" she said at last.

He looked startled by the question. Checking his pocket watch, he shook his head.

"I shall head back. I am sorry for troubling you. I am happy to see you are well." He bowed his head and left the room. "I shall tell Eloise as well," he added as an afterthought.

Once more Sarah found herself alone, but this time her mind was whirling with Thorne's strange behaviour.

She watched him leave, perplexed, before sitting down to write letters to her sister, Maria, and Mr. Featherston. A note had arrived, inviting her to his family estate for lunch. She had hesitated about accepting it; she knew not only what other people thought of him but what conclusions they would draw.

He was the first man she had found herself able to keep a correspondence and conversation with. He was easy to talk to and funnily enough reminded her a lot of Maria.

For the next few days she was kept busy putting together baskets of goods to be handed out at the parish church. She also searched through her closet to find clothes that could be donated to be altered.

Eloise was recovering at home. Her energy had returned, but her uncle was worried that she might have a relapse. Even her husband wrote her a letter asking her to take care of herself.

Mr. Thorne had been successful at keeping her from trying to plan any more social gathering or parties. Neighbours called on them but, using Eloise's precarious health as an excuse, they did not return the visit. The price he had paid for this was in agreeing to let Miss Glousen stay on.

Sarah had not had any further run-ins with her, but she had also made it her business to avoid her.

Mr. Thorne had softened towards her considerably, though she had never gotten to the bottom of his randomly checking in on her.

She had taken to walking to Mrs. Greencroft's house with supplies and found the three-mile walk there and back enjoyable. It was on one of these walks that Mr. Thorne came across her.

He came to a sudden stop upon seeing her coming down the lane, pulling on the reins of his horse.

"Lady Askew, how do you do?"

"I am well. On my way to Mrs. Greencroft," she said, holding up the basket for him to see.

He was looking at her in that peculiar way of his. "Are you alone? Should your maid not have come with you?"

"She usually does, but they are trying to clean out the house today and I did not wish to trouble her. The roads are quite safe. This isn't the first time I have made this walk," Sarah said, trying to assure him.

He did not seem to believe her, and to her shock he dismounted in one graceful motion.

He walked over to her, leading his horse by its reins.

"Are you planning on accompanying me?" she asked, unable to keep the surprise from her voice. "I really do not wish to trouble you."

"It is no trouble, Lady Askew," he said. "I could not leave you to walk the rest of the way unescorted. It would be against my honour."

She gave him what she hoped didn't seem to be a condescending look.

"You are quite the chevalier. But truly—"

"The sooner we get there, the less time you will be keeping me from my work," he pointed out. "So, you see, it is in your best interest to humour me and let me see you safely home."

Seeing how stubborn he was prepared to be, she relented, and they began walking. It was a lovely autumn day; a carpet of golden leaves littered the side of the road, the sun shone brightly, and yet it was not overly warm.

The sound of a carriage coming up from behind them made them pause and turn to see who it was.

Sarah, seeing Mr. Featherston in a carriage sitting next to an older woman she assumed was his mother, waved to him. As she did so, she caught Mr. Thorne's downcast expression and had to wonder why he seemed to disapprove of Mr. Featherston so much.

The carriage stopped, and all greetings and necessary introductions were made.

"It is a pleasure to meet you, Lady Askew. I have heard many good things about you. Mrs. Reed visited me the other day and could only talk about what a charitable, active young lady you were. I hope you have accepted our invitation to luncheon," Mrs. Featherston said.

"Yes, I have," Sarah said, bowing her head. She was still not comfortable accepting compliments. "I look forward to the visit. Thank you for the invitation."

"It was my son who pressed for it, but I see you have been a good influence on him," Mrs. Featherston said, pointing her parasol towards him as though she was accusing him of something. "You are welcome to join us as well, Mr. Thorne, if you are available," she said, turning her attention to Mr. Thorne.

He straightened up upon being addressed. "If business does not prevent me. I have been very busy, though it is my greatest wish."

"Yes, you have your hands full, or so I hear. A house full of women. However do you manage?" Mrs. Featherston said with a laugh. "Well, we must be off. Good day."

"Good day," Sarah called after them, with a secret smile to Mr. Featherston who rolled his eyes when his mother wasn't looking.

The driver clicked to the horses and urged them forward.

"A very pleasant woman," she said, trying to probe Thorne into conversation.

He grunted in reply but seemed more than happy to continue in silence.

"Pleasant weather too."

"He's a very young sort of man. From all reports, very idle and seems to not have a very clear path of where he wants life to take him."

Sarah wasn't expecting this, and it made her stop walking for a moment so that she had to quicken her step to catch up to him.

"Are you speaking of Mr. Featherston?"

"Yes," came the curt reply.

It was then Sarah remembered something Miss Glousen had said about the jealousy of men. She had waved it away at the time as foolishness, and it was true that Miss Glousen was simply trying to goad her at the time, but seeing Mr. Thorne's behaviour now made her think there was at least a kernel of truth in this.

"Mr. Featherston is misunderstood. I have spent a few lovely afternoons in his company now..."

"It has not passed my notice," Mr. Thorne said, his gaze fixed on the road ahead. He was doing a good job of avoiding eye contact with her.

Sarah bit her lip to stop herself from doing something foolish like laugh or exclaim in surprise.

"He is lonely," she said, trying to find some way to explain to him without jumping to conclusions. Knowing Mr. Thorne as well as she did, she knew he would not take it kindly if she accused him of being jealous outright, but she also wanted to settle his fears. Then she wondered why he would be jealous at all. It could not be that he liked her. No, that would be preposterous. But perhaps he was worried about her marrying and wasting the fortune she was given or, even worse, if her new husband took up residence at the cottage.

She supposed that, like all people, he did not take her seriously when she said she did not wish to remarry. Or at least had no inclination to do so.

He laughed. "Yes, I imagine he is. How lucky for him that he has found a willing friend in you."

"I keep repeating myself to you, Mr. Thorne. I am not a fool. I am a good judge of character. You should not listen to rumours and let your imagination get the better of you. Mr. Featherston is a serious man who is just trying to find his place in the world. He puts on a facade and enjoys making conversation. I am not surprised it has drawn the attention of some and led to tongues wagging," she said, a bit exasperated with him.

"I don't think you are a fool." He spoke so softly that she had barely heard him. "Very well, I shall not speak of him again. I have said my piece."

She opened her mouth to argue with him when she suddenly found herself falling, a gasp escaping her lips. She closed her eyes, fearing the impact, but it never came.

"I've got you," she heard Mr. Thorne's voice, full of concern, say.

He had caught her around the middle. She opened her eyes, flustered and embarrassed by her clumsiness. She looked behind her to see that she had tripped over a tree root. She was flattered by the very real concern she saw in his face and even more so that he had acted so quickly.

She couldn't help but notice that he needed to shave; a light stubble covered his chin, but it made him look handsome. She wondered what he would look like with a beard and flushed that such thoughts would pass through her head as he set her on her feet, releasing his hold on her.

"Thank you," she said, avoiding his gaze.

"You ought to be more careful when you walk," he said with a cough to clear his throat.

They walked on in silence for a while before Sarah had the courage to speak again.

"Even if he were to propose to me I would not say yes."

"I..." His mouth was hanging open at her frankness.

He smiled at her. "You surprise me sometimes. I forget how you like to goad me."

She returned the smile with her own. "Admit that you enjoy being kept on your toes."

He tilted his head. "I suppose it depends on who's doing it."

A sense of happiness passed through her at his words.

"And Eloise, how is she getting on? I should visit more often, but I am afraid I am unwanted."

He looked at her with concern. "You are always welcome. She speaks so highly of how well you took care of her. If it is to Miss Glousen you are referring, then say the word and she shall be gone."

Sarah shook her head. Despite the fact this was indeed what she desired. "Eloise cares for her too."

"I know; I should have taken that into consideration with the way I acted towards her."

She sneaked a sidelong glance at him and could see how pensive he looked.

"I know something of your history with her. She mentioned that she had been acquainted with my late husband."

To his credit, he did not falter in his step or look shocked.

"She is a special sort of woman, I am learning. Very single-minded in pursuing what she wants. I once found her charming, but I will never forget—once the fog was lifted—that she is not the sort of person I would wish to settle down with."

"I am happy that you are not heartbroken. If you pardon me for saying so."

He did not say anything, and, thinking to make the conversation lighter, she couldn't help but inquire, "And what sort of person would you wish to settle down with?"

He gave her a look. "I believe I should maintain an air of mystery about some things."

Chuckling, she agreed to let him keep his secrets.

They reached Mrs. Greencroft's house. A large two-storey building built in red brick.

She knocked on the door and was surprised that Mrs. Greencroft herself opened the door, wearing an apron.

"Good afternoon, Lady Askew," she said, then catching Mr. Thorne waiting behind her, smiled and nodded to him too. "Mr. Thorne, what brings you to my doorstep?"

"I was escorting Lady Askew. I did not think it would be good for her to walk alone," he said.

"You thought correctly. I am always pleased to see a young person look out for such things. Shall I invite you all inside for something to eat?"

Sarah shook her head.

"I just came to drop these off," she said, handing her the basket of apples and cabbages from her kitchen. "I am afraid I am keeping Mr. Thorne from his work and I dare not delay him any further."

"So considerate. Be careful you don't lose yourself while trying to take care of others," Mrs. Greencroft said, leaning closer to her so they couldn't be overheard.

Sarah laughed off her comment. "I am hardly at risk of doing that. Good day."

They began the long walk back, letting Mr. Thorne's horse stop to graze on the greenery along the path.

"She is a very nice woman," Sarah commented. "I do not know many people quite so charitable as her."

Mr. Thorne nodded. "She comes from a peculiar background. Her mother was a laundress and her father a baron."

"Oh?" Sarah was surprised.

"It's common gossip. If you were the sort to concern yourself over such matters, then you would know. But I agree with you, she is very nice. She and Mr. Greencroft have been happily married for many years. Her children have grown and married, but the stain of her past still follows her."

"Just as I am the cursed bride?" she said, thinking back to the newspaper articles.

"Yes, but I hope you shall not be forever censured because of that," he said, looking at her with something akin to pity in his eyes.

"That is why you need not be concerned. I am more than happy to live out my days in my current state, and if you are lucky, you shall outlive me and see your estate intact again."

He stopped in his tracks. "Don't say such things."

She felt like she was being reprimanded, and it was true she had spoken out of turn and rather hastily.

"Forgive me, I know you do not wish me ill. You have been nothing but kind. You take better care of me than I do of myself. I am grateful," she said to him, feeling subdued.

"Lady Askew..."

She looked up, meeting his dark eyes with her own. The intensity she saw there made her suddenly uncertain of herself.

Sarah didn't know what to make of it, so she did the only thing she felt comfortable doing and continued walking. He followed suit, a step or two behind her, like a shadow dogging her steps.

Why were all their interactions a series of misunderstandings that usually culminated in her misspeaking.

At church the following week, Sarah put on her Sunday best and rode in the carriage, squeezed between Miss Glousen and Eloise. Mr. Thorne had gone back to avoiding her company, and she had not felt comfortable sitting so close to him. If the other of their party had noticed, they did not say a word.

They took their seats at church and waited for the parson to begin his sermon.

Sarah was not listening to him, as she was playing over in her mind what she would say to Mrs. Rodes. She settled on something more subtle, an olive branch. At first her inclination had been to approach her in public, but she knew that would be far from the correct course of action to take. Mrs. Rodes might agree, but she would forever hate her after that.

Sarah pulled her aside as the congregation was leaving. A penitent smile on her face.

"May I call on you the day after tomorrow?"

Mrs. Rodes nodded. "To what may I owe this honour?"

"I wish to ask you for your help, and I am afraid to do so with everyone present," Sarah said, keeping her voice piteously low.

Mrs. Rodes, the self-assured woman that she was, agreed right away. "Of course, you may always confide in me."

Sarah gave her a bright smile. "I knew you would be understanding. Thank you very much."

"Not to worry, Lady Askew."

Sarah left to go find Mr. Thorne and the rest of the party, a self-pleased air about herself, when Mr. Featherston caught up to her and began walking beside her.

"How do you do?" he said, tilting his hat to her.

"Oh very well, making my move so to speak," Sarah said, confiding in him.

"Oh? What are you planning?"

"Nothing exciting, I am afraid, but hopefully something to help my friends," Sarah said, whispering now so they wouldn't be overheard.

"You will have to tell me about it tomorrow," Mr. Featherston said with a grin.

They had reached her party, and he bid them all good morning. Mr. Thorne could only manage a gruff hello in his direction. Something that Mr. Featherston must have found amusing, for he gave Sarah a secret smile.

As they got into the carriage, Miss Glousen suggested that Sarah sit beside Mr. Thorne.

"You cannot have anything to worry about, Lady Askew," Miss Glousen said, seeing her hesitation. "There is nothing wrong with sitting beside a man. If you are concerned the parson is right there..."

Sarah bit the inside of her cheek to keep from saying something she'd regret.

"I am sure you'd much rather sit with him, Miss Glousen," she said.

"Lady Askew, just get in or I'll make all of you walk home." Mr. Thorne had seemingly heard everything and looked both irritated and tired all at once.

Sarah did not argue and took her seat, her gaze fixed out the window. She tried not to take notice as he sat on her right. She tried not to notice when his shoulder brushed hers or when the carriage jolted them, causing her leg to bump into his.

Across from her Miss Glousen seemed very amused but did not comment other than prompting Eloise to admit this was much more comfortable.

Eloise could only nod. She was focusing on not throwing up as the jolting was making her nauseous, and she kept a hand to her belly as though to support herself and her growing child.

Sarah noted how much bigger she seemed. It had been two months since she arrived; she must be approaching her sixth or seventh month.

They arrived at the house without any further delay,

and Eloise was kind enough to invite her to stay for dinner.

"The cook promised me a roast duck," she said, with all the glee of a hungry child being given candy.

So Sarah could not refuse her.

The ladies retreated to the drawing room, newly wallpapered and freshly painted. It was tastefully decorated with vases and new screens laid about the room. A piano forte was set up in the corner and Eloise, impatient, decided to try to play for them while they waited.

Mr. Thorne had disappeared to his reclaimed office.

Sarah tried to make a mental note of all the transformations the house had undergone. Her sister Louisa would be particularly curious—it seemed she had taken to decorating, rearranging furniture, and moving pieces around to create a more aesthetically pleasing room. Her mother had written of it, brimming with pride as she saw this as something worthy of praise, but was quick to follow up with the fact she was just as wild as ever. Her mother never wrote to ask her how she did but rather to give her news of the family in such a way that she would regret staying away, and her not so subtle prodding for her to return was an ever-present irritation to Sarah. She had already promised to make the journey for Christmas, even though as the time approached she found herself regretting that promise.

"Do you like what I have done with that arrangement over there?" Miss Glousen said, over the music.

Sarah looked in the direction she was pointing. "Yes. You have an eye for such things," she said.

"Mr. Thorne sent to London for the peacock feathers for me," she let her know with a certain smile.

"That was very kind of him." Sarah had grown bored and moved to the bookcase lining the far wall to investigate if there was a book that struck her fancy. She also hoped Miss Glousen would take the hint. She wasn't interested in a fight.

"When will you be able to enter half-mourning?"

Sarah, distracted by the spines of the books, looked towards her. "In a fortnight or so. I haven't thought about it."

"You must be very excited to be out of that black. You sour everyone's mood whenever you walk by. One cannot help but think of death coming when one sees you. I daresay you would improve everyone's mood if you laid it away."

CLANG

Eloise had slammed her fingers on the piano keys.

They were silent as they watched her. Sarah had a hand pressed to her heart—she had been startled out of her wits.

"Why must you always be so mean and pick a fight?" Eloise was glaring at Miss Glousen. She began playing from where she left off.

Sarah turned back to the books to hide a smile. She was happy to see that Eloise had not only said something to her friend but had stood up for her.

The housekeeper came to let them know that dinner would be ready soon. The other two ladies went to their rooms to change, but Sarah, who had not thought it worth the bother of returning home, would stay in the dress she wore at church. After all, it was one of her best dresses. What did it matter to her what she looked like? And as Miss Glousen had pointed out, regardless of the shape of the dress she would look like death.

"Ah, you are in here."

Sarah looked up to find Mr. Thorne in the doorway, surprised to have come upon her.

"Please, don't let me get in your way," she said. "I was just reading until dinner is ready."

"You aren't," he said. "That is to say, it is a pleasure to have you dining with us. I just came here for a book. I haven't installed shelves in my office yet, so I have been keeping my own books here."

"I was wondering why there were so many agricultural books among the poetry," Sarah said with a teasing smile.

"Yes..." He coughed. "Well, I..." Then an idea seemed to strike him. "Would you like to see my office? And the ballroom? I finally found a place for that obnoxious chandelier. I was wondering if I could have your opinion on it."

She agreed to go, setting her book aside with a bookmark.

Sarah followed after him, listening to him talk animatedly about all the improvements he had made and the plans that were still to be put into action.

"You must fix up the pavilion in the woods too. It was so lovely," she said when he had stopped long enough for her to speak.

"The pavilion? That's all ruins now. You went there?"

She nodded. "It was very beautiful. The ruins add a magical sort of feeling to it. You could turn it into a fairy garden."

"Who took you there?"

Sarah could see a shadow cross his face.

They had reached his office. She entered the room, admiring the desk and the general layout of the room.

"Very practical," she said, not able to look him in the eye quite yet.

"You never answered me."

She found herself swallowing hard, suddenly aware of his presence and how alone they were. Her eyes widened and she stepped out of the room, but his hand slinked around her wrist, forbidding her from leaving. Her breath hitched in her chest.

"Lady Askew, you should not be alone in the woods with strangers."

"I told you, he is no stranger, and you need not reprimand me," she said as she tugged her wrist away from his grasp, and as though realizing what he had done, he let her go as though she was a hot coal he had touched.

"You are still so naive. Not everyone has the best of intentions, and that is a very secluded part of the woods. No one would hear you if you needed help. I am just thinking—"

"Of my well-being. I know. You are always saying that," she said rather coldly. "My maid was there if you are so concerned, but why would you even care? You have always made it clear that I am little more than an annoyance."

"You are under my protection." Mr. Thorne was looking away from her now. She did the same, wondering why his words made her heart flutter. It wasn't the sentiment, which was the usual response, but the way he had said it.

"Mr. Thorne..."

But the rest of her words caught in her throat; his hand had travelled to her face, moving a stray strand of hair out of her face.

He cleared his throat. "Shall I show you the ballroom?"

Sarah watched him turn away and disappear down the corridor. She had a few moments to collect herself. What had just happened? She couldn't be sure. She knew little of the ways of men, but she did not think Mr. Thorne was the type to make advances. Sarah stopped her train of thought. She was being ridiculous. Even if he did like her, hadn't she decided that marriage was not in her future?

She caught up to him, hoping that her cheeks were not burning red.

"I see what you mean about the chandelier," she said. "It does look much better here."

The curtains were pulled back, showing off the greenery of the countryside through the large windows. In the centre of the room hung that horrid piece. She could tell that he had had it altered somewhat, removing one layer of crystals.

They caught the light beautifully. She noticed that the sconces on the wall had all received a little crystal of their own. She was pleasantly surprised. She could just imagine this room in the evening, the soft candlelight, the musicians, garlands hanging about the room. It would be beautiful.

"I thought, later, we might throw a ball. Perhaps next summer, once it would be appropriate for you to dance again," he said.

Sarah found her throat had gone dry.

"That is considerate of you," she said.

"Of course, I can't imagine that Eloise will be with us for much longer. I should have you play the part of hostess. Her husband has assured me he will have her settled in her own home before the baby arrives."

"He must move quickly then," she said. There were only a few months to go. "I hope she will not move far."

"Not very far, I should think." Mr. Thorne spun around, heading for the double doors.

"Mr. Thorne..."

But by the time he turned around she had lost her nerve.

"Thank you for showing me the ballroom."

Sarah had trouble sleeping that night. All she could wonder was why he had behaved so strangely towards her. Why had he gotten so close? She found it so strange to think that he might admire her in that way. She had always regarded women like Maria or even Miss Glousen the type of women that drew men's admiration.

She imagined herself married to him and flushed at the thought. No, it was ridiculous to even speculate. He was just looking out for her. Some foolish part of him had made him think that he needed to.

CHAPTER EIGHT

The next morning she had dark circles under her eyes. She hoped when she reached the Featherston's home that she would not look quite so pale and exhausted, more ready for her sickbed than for lunch.

She was greeted with particular attention by his mother, who took the time to show her around the main floor herself. They lingered at a portrait of her eldest son.

"Albert is at Bath at present for the health of his wife. She is as dear to me as my own daughter, but I am afraid she has been having trouble," Mrs. Featherston said. "My Albert is so considerate and generous and whisked her away from us."

"Yes, he is awfully kind. A pity he did not think of my health as well," Mr. George Featherston said, with a smile to Sarah as he adjusted his cravat. "Lovely to see you again, Lady Askew."

"And where have you been all morning?" Mrs. Featherston reprimanded her younger son. "You invite guests and leave me to entertain them for you?"

He held up his hands in apology. "I was detained in town."

She snorted. "Settling your accounts?"

"Yes, Mother. Please don't embarrass me in front of my guests."

Mrs. Featherston seemed to remember that Sarah was there and flushed. "Well, she might as well know. The whole town will know soon enough."

"What is it?" Sarah asked, intrigued.

"Have you shown her the gardens?"

"No..."

"Then allow me to escort you, Lady Askew. Mother, you may come too of course," he said.

She frowned. "I'll wait for you in the parlour. Don't dawdle too long. Lady Askew, I warn you away from this deviant."

With a flurry of skirts she was gone.

Sarah was trying to stifle a laugh. It was rare to see such genuine family emotion.

"Excuse my mother. She is touchy about me lately," Mr. Featherston said, offering her his arm, which she took eagerly.

"Do tell me all about what business you had in town."

He laughed. "It was my latest attempt at escape. I was persuaded to invest foolishly, and the venture failed. So I lost the little pocket money I had."

Sarah placed a hand over his. Despite his humour she knew it struck him deeply. It was not surprising to see, considering how doting his mother seemed to be towards his older brother.

"You must put it out of your mind," she said. "Something will come along. I'll find you a rich heiress, and the two of you will fall madly in love with each other."

"If only it could be so easy," he said but seemed cheered. "Thank you for joining me today. I do have another confession."

"What?"

"Well, my mother is under the impression I am courting you."

"You cannot be serious!" Sarah was flabbergasted.

He was adjusting his cufflinks, abashed at himself. "I did not correct her. Not because it is the truth but because for the first time in a long time she approves of something I am doing."

Sarah didn't know what to say.

"I don't have any such designs on you," he hurried to say, seeing how concerned she was. "I do think of you as a friend and a wonderful change to an otherwise dreary social life here in Bluehaven."

Sarah breathed out a sigh of relief, though she wasn't sure she was happy with this master plan of his.

"You cannot keep tricking her. If you want her to take you seriously, you should be honest with her."

He kicked at some stones along the path. "It is more complicated than that. I am the black sheep of the family."

"You shall have to repair your reputation, and the first thing you can do is take yourself more seriously. No more foolish investments. No more dallying with widows and telling your mother you are pursuing them if you are not. What if my feelings were hurt?"

He looked terribly sorry then, having not considered that. "You aren't hurt, are you?"

"No," she said, shaking her head. "I know you were having a bit of fun. It was amusing, though I did feel flattered."

"Good, you deserve it. Come this way, and then I shall let you continue to scold me," he said.

He led her down a path not far from the house. A long row of hedges fenced off a large section of the garden; he opened a wooden gate and motioned her to step inside.

It was a beautiful maze. The hedges inside only came up to her hips. Flowers were interspersed among the paths. At the centre she could see a fountain and two benches.

"This is lovely, Mr. Featherston," she said.

They walked through, weaving in and out of the pathways.

After a time she noticed that some of the paved stones had words carved into them. Sarah stopped to examine one, reading the poetry on it.

"Who wrote these?"

Mr. Featherston grinned. "I did. What do you think? My mother planned out the hedge maze, but I saw to this little detail. She found it too romantic for her taste, but this is just the sort of thing this dreary old place needs."

"Yes, perfect for making unsuspecting widows fall in love with you."

"Oh? And are you in danger, Lady Askew? Tell me now so I may run the other way."

She laughed. "Every time I come close to it, you open your mouth and send me running off."

He clutched his palms to his chest. "You've struck me deep. You must call for a doctor."

"Hush, now. Let me read," she said, turning her attention back to the poems.

Every few steps there was a new stanza.

It told the tale of love, from its beginnings, and at the very centre of the maze was its end. It was a bittersweet poem and it filled her with a strange sort of longing. An image of Mr. Thorne floated to the forefront of her mind. Sarah remembered how Mr. Featherston had spoken of Roselyn, the daughter who met a tragic end at Oakham.

"How did she die?"

He seemed to know exactly who she was referring to. "She took ill one summer and never recovered. They took her to London to see the best physician, but she never returned. I never got to say goodbye."

She wanted to help him somehow and make all the hurt and worries go away. He was not the cheerful care-free man he pretended to be.

"The way she's still in your memory would honour anyone," Sarah said at last, wondering if anyone could love her as much as it seemed Mr. Featherston did Roselyn.

"Even if she had lived, I don't think we could have

ever been together. Her parents would not have thought me good enough for her. We enjoyed talking of eloping to Gretna Green, but of course, I could never dishonour her by eloping."

"Try not to dwell on it," she said. "You would have found a way. But regardless, I doubt she would want you to spend your remaining days on earth in such a sad state. You have some skill with the pen; perhaps you should consider making writing your career," she said, turning to him.

He had been following behind her in silent contemplation.

From his sly expression she knew she had discovered a secret.

"You must tell me; it is the least you could do for your future wife." She chuckled, seeing how he had nearly choked on whatever he had to say next.

"Now who's the flirt?" he said after he managed to clear his throat. "I have sent a few things to be published anonymously. But I haven't told my family. I am not eager to face their commentary or for them to forbid me to continue."

"They wouldn't. You write very well—there is no shame in it," she said.

"I am sure they would have preferred me to go into the church," he said, taking a seat on a bench.

She sat across from him, mesmerized by the way the water in the fountain caught the sun's rays.

"Is that why you put up this pretence of being a shameless flirt with ladies?"

"You are too clever," he said, shifting the hat on his head.

With the sun beating down on them and no shade, Sarah felt compelled to open her parasol. It was autumn and she had to layer her dress against the cold. It didn't mean that she couldn't burn.

"I am glad we crossed each other's path. For once I feel like the wise old crone I pretend to be," she said.

He looked at her as though he were studying her. "Unless you were very adept at magic and make-up then I doubt you are hiding an old crone under there. Enough about me. Tell me, how are things at your cottage?"

"Well enough," she said, twirling the parasol.

"Hmm. And your Mr. Thorne? Is he still in the claws of Miss Glousen?"

"No, I believe he has never been."

He gave her a wink. "He would have been a fool to have fallen for her wiles."

"You seemed to have picked up on them quite easily," she said. "Or at the very least you never seemed taken with her."

"She was nice, and beautiful, I cannot deny it, but if I had started flirting with her then I am afraid she would have taken me all too seriously. She is a woman on the hunt for a husband, and I am terrified of such creatures."

She gave him a disapproving look.

"What, am I wrong?" He raised his eyebrow in challenge. "Besides, once she would discover I am the mere second son, I doubt she would even look twice at me."

"Oh, I suspect she knows enough about you. She bothered to warn me off," she said with a grin.

"She did? Hmm, I am surprised. She must not be quite so cold-hearted as you think. Otherwise, she would have been more than happy to encourage you and get you out of the way."

"What do you mean by that?"

"Mr. Thorne. She sees you as the...competition. But it is hardly a competition." He tilted his head towards her. "In disposition and composure there is none other here that can compete with you."

"Now, don't be silly," Sarah said, flushing.

"Mr. Thorne doesn't strike me as the sort of man to be taken in by feminine charms and manipulations. You are charming in your sincerity and at times even your obliviousness."

"You misunderstand him. The two of us have never been on very good terms."

"I see the way he looks at you. The way he shoots daggers in my direction every time I get too close. I think he is in danger of falling for you, and you don't even realize it. That is part of your allure."

"Let's talk about your poetry again," she said, ready to jump off this topic. She was distracted for the rest of the visit.

Even as they ate lunch and she was served plate after plate of extravagant dishes. She complimented each and every one of them but did not have much appetite. She also glared at Mr. Featherston from time to time. Clearly, his mother had gone out of her way to please her on behalf of her son, with the view that soon she might become her daughter-in-law.

As she said goodbye, she made him promise her to correct his parents.

"Only if you convince Mr. Thorne to restore that pavilion," he said in a whisper.

She frowned. "If I could, I would ship it over to you piece by piece. You seem to care for it so much."

He had a far-off look on his face. "It was my favourite place in all the world and where Roselyn confessed she loved me."

She touched his sleeve, wishing more than anything to have some way to comfort him.

"Live for her if not for yourself. You never know what the future will bring. I certainly could not have predicted any of this," she said, making a sweeping gesture with her hand.

His mother was approaching and quickly he put on a false smile.

"Very well, Lady Askew. I shall do what you asked once I hear of your own success," he said, flashing her a mischievous smile.

She frowned slightly but forced herself to be genial before turning to his mother.

"Thank you for your hospitality, Mrs. Featherston."

"Nonsense, one is happy to be welcoming of new neighbours." She rushed to reassure Sarah.

On the way home in the borrowed carriage, Sarah couldn't help but speculate about everything that was said between herself and Mr. Featherston. In a way, things would have been simpler if she were indeed interested in him and him in her. But it was not to be.

She was eager to pay a call on Eloise that evening, but she remembered she had to prepare for her visit to Mrs. Rodes the very next day. It was lucky that she had started keeping a schedule, otherwise she would have forgotten for sure.

Her personal matters could wait; she had more important things to think about.

She pulled out a fresh sheet of paper and began writing out a few calculations and making a list of items to bring to Mrs. Rodes' attention.

She would have to make everything as easy as possible for her, otherwise she might never agree. Mrs. Greencroft was relying on her to see this through.

Bright and early the next morning, Sarah dressed with careful attention to her hair and clothes. She wore a brooch of black jade on her dress but no other adornment besides the gold cross she usually wore around her neck.

Her maid fussed with her hair saying she should curl the front, but Sarah, knowing that Mrs. Rodes was particular and had specific expectations of widows, left it straight and plain. In fact, she had her maid part her hair down the centre and pull it back, creating quite a severe effect when coupled with the black bonnet.

She started the long walk to the parsonage, which was within sight of the parish church.

She had wrapped a heavy cloak around her to protect her from the chilly autumn day. October was coming to an end and that much was clear.

She reached the Rodes' residence and knocked.

Sarah didn't have to wait long, but every second made her feel as though her heart was pounding with increasing anxiety.

"Hello, Miss...Who are you?" A short plump woman said, answering the door.

"Can you please tell your mistress that Lady Askew is here to see her?"

"Of course. Pardon me, Lady Askew," the servant said, giving her a small curtsey.

She was left standing outside the door, feeling a bit like a beggar, until the servant returned and opened the door wide enough for her to pass through.

"Please come in, Lady Askew. She's expecting you," she said, all politeness.

Sarah followed her to the drawing room on the east side of the house. The room was small but filled with the very best of things, from newly upholstered chairs, mahogany cabinets, with all sorts of trinkets on display.

Mrs. Rodes stood, though delayed this show of courtesy just long enough for her to be sure Sarah had noticed how begrudgingly she had done it.

"Thank you for having me," Sarah said, still standing awkwardly in the middle of the room.

"You are very welcome. Can I offer you some tea? I am afraid it won't be as fine as anything you are used to, but I make do."

Sarah smiled, debating whether it would be worse to accept it or refuse. "Thank you, I would be happy for some."

"Take a seat," Mrs. Rodes said at last.

Sarah, happy for the rest after the long walk, complied eagerly.

The maid left, presumably to fetch the tea.

"So, tell me what it is you wished to speak to me about?"

Sarah smiled; this woman did not dally about, talking circles before finally getting to the point. "I couldn't help but notice how many less fortunate people are part of our congregation here. I know with the cold weather and winter approaching many would be hard pressed to make ends meet."

"It is our burden to bear our lot in life."

"Of course, I am not one to argue on such matters. I had wondered if you had planned to do anything for them at Christmas? I would wish to help in any way I can. I know that others are active in charitable giving, but I always thought this should be from the parish church itself, and as the parson's wife—"

"We do not neglect our flock. We feed as many as we can from the funds we receive." Mrs. Rodes was getting defensive.

Luckily the tea arrived.

Sarah had to take a breath and then start again. "Of course, I am sure you and your husband are doing all you can. I wondered how I may help to do more. I need no credit. If you were to throw a dinner, let's say, it would be the talk of the town. I am sure the news of your good deeds would circulate everywhere. Maybe there would even be a column in the lady's paper about it. You'd be an example to us all. I know how busy you are, and that is why I wished to be of aid to you. I drew up a list of what I could provide and the costs I could cover," she said, pulling it out of her pocket and handing it to the suspicious-looking woman.

"Why would you not plan a dinner yourself?" Mrs. Rodes asked.

Sarah hesitated before answering. "It is not my place to involve myself in such an open way with something like this. The credit should go to where it rightfully belongs." She stared at her pointedly. "Besides, my family has demanded my presence for Christmas, so I would not be able to look after affairs."

"Then who would help me?"

Sarah hid a smile by taking a sip of tea. "There are several parish wives who would be more than happy to help. Have you thought of Mrs. Greencroft or Mrs. Reed? They are very kind and involved in all sorts of charitable works."

"Hmm." She seemed to be very tempted by all of this. She was looking down at the list Sarah had drawn up, calculating what she would have to cover.

"We could hold a donation for the dinner," Sarah added. "I am sure many would be generous around this time of year."

She continued sipping at the tea, which was a bit

strong for her liking but she dared not ask for more milk or sugar. At last, Mrs. Rodes spoke.

"I can see I might have been mistaken about you. You seem to have a very generous heart. You know how things should be done. Unlike others..." Her serious expression cracked with a smile of her own. "I agree to your terms."

Sarah felt elated.

"Whatever I can help with, please let me know. Until I leave I shall be at your disposal."

This seemed to give Mrs. Rodes a sense of satisfaction. A lady at her beck and call.

She thanked her kindly enough.

They sat together a while longer, talking about the weather, and the news from London that the king had fallen ill again. Finally it was time for her to depart.

Sarah's walk home was much more relaxing than her walk to the parsonage had been. She had a spring in her step and even hummed a tune. That was how Mr. Thorne came across her as she was walking down the lane towards the main house.

Embarrassed, she curtseyed to him.

"Good afternoon, Mr. Thorne."

"Good day to you as well, Lady Askew. Though I do not think I need to ask how you do," he said.

She smiled. "I didn't see you, or I would have stopped."

"Being happy or singing?"

"Just the singing," she said, looking at the ground. "I was told by a music master that I have a grating voice and cannot hold a tune. I would not have wanted you to be subjected to it."

When she looked up again, she could see him frowning as he studied her with that intense gaze of his.

"I cannot decide if you are fishing for compliments or not, but let me assure you that your voice is far from grating."

She licked her lips. "Thank you, I am less embarrassed knowing that."

"How was your outing? I see you went out alone again unaccompanied.'

"I walked to the parish church, and as you can see I am fine. I did not encounter a handsome prince to escort me this time," she said jokingly.

He seemed amused, and even managed to smile.

"You are incorrigible. I suppose you left by the side gate, so I could not have seen you and caught up to you too," he said, shaking his head.

She grinned. "I might have, but what's it to you? And yes, I know I am under your protection," she said as she walked past him. "You might have to resort to locking me up and throwing away the key."

It was then she realized she had miscalculated; she had passed by too closely to him, giving him the opportunity to grasp her hand.

He did not hold it tightly, but it stopped her in her tracks just the same.

While maintaining eye contact, he brought her hand to his lips.

"Don't tempt me," he said, his expression coy.

She did not pull away her hand, even as he brought her hand up to his lips, kissing the back of her palm.

She pulled away. "I shall not be scared away by your tricks."

"Tricks?"

"Yes," Sarah said, rubbing the hand that had been kissed as though she was rubbing away the kiss itself. "You always think you can silence me with your touches and caresses, but I have caught on to what you are doing."

He took a step closer to her, leaning in. "And what, pray tell, am I doing?"

"Intimidating me," she said, straightening up.

He pulled back, laughing. "You amuse me, Lady Askew. I am sorry you think that is what I am doing and even more sorry if I have behaved improperly."

"Good day, Mr. Thorne," Sarah said, without another word. Trying her best not to appear like a complete ingénue.

As she walked back to her cottage, her irritation with him grew with each step. If he had behaved improperly? She could laugh. If her brother was old enough, he would have challenged him to a duel if he had come across them in the library, his hand on her face like that. It didn't help that the way he made her feel confused her so much. She wished she could get a hold of herself. She hated how weak she felt whenever he was around, as though she yearned for him to pull her into his arms. That was foolishness.

She swore to herself that she would never read another novel again. Especially one of a romantic nature;

they had corrupted her. She resolved to write a strongly worded letter to Maria, who would bear the brunt of her anger, since Mr. Thorne seemed uncooperative in that regard. She thought of the jokes Mr. Featherston had made at their expense. She wanted to prove these people wrong...not right.

She had the urge to stomp her feet and kick around like she had seen her sister do when she was younger.

It was lucky for her that she had contained herself. Coming up the path from her cottage were Miss Glousen and Eloise, hand in hand.

"There you are," Eloise called out. "We have just come up from the cottage. Your housekeeper said you had left early this morning. I am glad we have caught you."

"I am sorry too. I should have told you I would be away. Hello, Miss Glousen," she said.

The woman in question seemed mesmerized, looking at her as though she wasn't quite sure what she was seeing.

"Good lord, Lady Askew. Who did your hair? You must dismiss them immediately," she said with a deep frown. "I would never leave the house looking like that. You are positively ridiculous."

Sarah was ready to laugh it off, acknowledging the truth of this, but Eloise had pulled away from her friend.

"I am growing tired of your comments. Why do you always feel compelled to speak so?"

"Mrs. Haverstock, please don't excite yourself," Sarah rushed in to stop her. "I am not offended. It is true I probably look ridiculous."

She flinched at the look Eloise gave her and backed away.

"I have found you most infuriating lately," Eloise said to Miss Glousen. "Please apologize to Lady Askew."

Miss Glousen looked taken aback but set aside her pride and did apologize. "I apologize for offending you, Lady Askew."

"I accept," Sarah said, rushing to do so. "See, Eloise, we are perfect friends now. Don't trouble yourself over me."

Eloise looked at her with a lot of sadness in her eyes. "You never wish to trouble anyone, and that should change. Let's go, Vicky," she said to her friend.

Sarah watched them walk off, puzzled and ill at ease. She hoped she would not be receiving another visit from Mr. Thorne telling her that Eloise had had a fit or fallen ill.

She had just finished writing a note to both Mrs. Greencroft and Mrs. Reed, telling them all about her exploits that morning and inviting them for tea on Thursday, when she spied Mr. Thorne walking up to the door of the cottage. Yet again she thanked her forethought in placing her writing desk where she had, or she might not have had warning.

He knocked, and her housekeeper opened the door.

Sarah stood, smoothing out her skirts and arranging her cap, but only the housekeeper came in carrying a note for her.

"Mr. Thorne dropped this off for you, ma'am," she said with a curtsey.

"Thank you." Sarah took it, trying to hide how her hands had begun shaking.

She waited until the woman had left the room before examining the note. The envelope was tied with twine. Upon opening it she saw a dried lilac inside. Gently she pulled it out, before setting it aside, her heart beating wildly in her chest. Lilacs were common for widows to wear as they stood for love, new and old. She let her fingers skim it as though she could read the intentions of the giver just from that.

She opened the note.

I hope you will forgive my imprudence in writing to you, but I must say it, as I feel that everyone but me shall catch on eventually. It is strange for me to write such things, but don't fear that I am about to write some dramatic declaration to you. You've asked me before why I seem so determined to protect you. I have not been entirely truthful with you. I hope you will burn this letter after you finish reading it, for I am mortified by what I must write since I cannot bear to say it to you face to face. I find myself drawn to you in ways that one might not consider suitable, given that you are the widow of my cousin. But there it is, I have said it. You need not say anything, or even reply, or even speak to me ever again. I shall say nothing further on the subject unless you speak first. I apologize for my previous behaviour to you, and I shall try to make amends.
Deepest regards,
Mr. William Thorne

Sarah realized that there were tears streaming down her cheeks as she read. There was something else tucked away in the envelope. She pulled out the scrap piece of paper. It was a sketch of herself sitting in the garden. He must have done this in the early months of her arrival, when he and Eloise had tea in the garden and they spent the day together. She blushed to think that he had studied her so closely to capture this image. He had been quite flattering in his portrayal of her, but that she would chalk up to artistic licence. After all, why would anyone draw a woman as she was.

She sat there rereading the letter over and over again. Wild thoughts crept into her mind.

Her maid came in to say that dinner was ready, but she asked for a plate to be brought up to her room. Sarah retreated to the warm security of her bed. The lilac was tucked away in the box of precious possessions on her nightstand. It was one of her most favourite flowers, though he had no way of knowing that unless he had been in her room.

She blushed as she remembered making an off-handed remark to Eloise in his presence about wishing to plant a lilac tree in her garden. She hadn't realized he was paying attention.

She gripped the letter to her chest, trying to calm herself.

Where could this relationship, if there was one to be had, even go? Would he propose marriage to her? She couldn't see that happening. How could she be sure he truly loved her and didn't simply see her as a way of getting a hold of the full value of the estate. After marriage, all she had would become his.

But then this letter...

He had never seemed like the devious sort to trick someone with such foolishness. Sarah bit her lip, catching her reflection in the mirror. She had removed her cap and most of the pins holding up that ridiculous hairdo, leaving her blonde hair free to frame her face in wavy curls. She had regular features, bright eyes, but nothing that she could call stunning.

She looked away but then forced herself to look back. She had to admit she was not the ugly old widow she had pictured in her head. Even if she was, would this make her unworthy of love? She would appreciate Mr. Thorne if he was not taken with her looks or wealth but rather herself for who she was. She had always been told she was not good enough, that her value lay in her youth and wealth. Her mind, personality, and aptitudes were not only unimportant but subpar. It was not just the music master that had implied this, but her mother, her governess, even at times her father. Hadn't he arranged her marriage believing that on her own she would be unable to attract the love and admiration of anyone?

Sarah felt fresh tears spring to her eyes, and she let them come, clinging to her knees as the sobs wracked her body.

When she had finished, she splashed cool water on her face from the wash-basin and looked at the letter again.

She wanted to talk to him. It would not do to leave

this, whatever it was, sitting between them. Tomorrow, when she had lunch with Eloise, she would give him a note of her own, one that might accomplish two things. After all, she had promised Mr. Featherston to get Mr. Thorne to consider repairing the pavilion.

She arrived at a house in uproar.

"Whatever is going on?" she asked the housekeeper who gave her a knowing smile.

"I am afraid Miss Glousen was asked to leave. A shame," she said, though Sarah got the impression she didn't mean the last part.

"Shall I go in or leave?"

"Mrs. Haverstock is in the drawing room until Miss Glousen leaves, and Mr. Thorne is in his office," the housekeeper said.

"Thank you, I shall go and see Mrs. Haverstock," Sarah said, wondering at the noise she heard upstairs. She got the impression Miss Glousen was shouting at some poor footman for not being careful with her things.

Eloise was lounging on a chaise, cocooned in a blanket while she flipped through a book rather absent-mindedly. She looked up when Sarah walked in, giving her a wide smile.

"Hello. I wasn't expecting you today. Will you join me? I'd stand, but I am too comfortable to move."

Sarah assured her she wouldn't dream of disturbing her.

She walked over, taking a seat beside her.

"What is happening?" Sarah asked, removing her bonnet.

"Miss Glousen has decided it would be best for her to leave," Eloise said with only the slightest hesitation.

"Is this on my behalf? Because I would not wish..."

But Eloise stopped her with one look. "Truth is, she is not the friend I remember. She has been so spiteful lately, and chasing after my uncle. She thought she was not being obvious about it, but I've known her for far too long to not notice. The way she treated you was the last straw. I hope we can mend our friendship. She still means a lot to me, but she is making me more stressed than I'd like to be," Eloise said rather firmly. "I am sure my uncle is thrilled. Have you seen him?"

Sarah shook his head.

"He's been in an awfully good mood, and then he shut himself in his office this morning. Probably wants to avoid seeing Vic—Miss Glousen."

"Shall I stay and read to you, so you don't strain your eyes?"

Eloise accepted her offer, and Sarah began where Eloise had left off. It was not long before her friend had fallen fast asleep. Sarah blamed her monotone voice when reading but thought she might take this chance to slip the note to Mr. Thorne's office.

She made her way there, careful to not look too inconspicuous. Luckily, most of the household had found little jobs to keep themselves occupied and out of the main house while Miss Glousen was vacating it.

She listened in at the closed door to make sure no one else was there. She couldn't hear anything, which also made her wonder if he was even in there. Sarah, having been assured of his location by both Eloise and the housekeeper, bent down to slip the letter under the door.

She should have prayed for luck because just then the door was opened and, startled, she had fallen on her backside. She must have painted a ridiculous picture and, like a child caught red-handed, she was too scared to look up, even as the concerned Mr. Thorne asked her if she was well.

"I apologize, Lady Askew, I had not expected to find you here."

"I am sorry...I should not have disturbed you. Goodbye."

Sarah had rushed to her feet and fled back down the corridor. She only stopped to let the housekeeper know she had some urgent business to attend to and left by the front door.

She hoped the letter hadn't gone amiss, but even if it had it was too late for her to turn around now. She bit her finger, debating as she walked what the outcome of this would be. Would he meet her tomorrow morning at the pavilion? Only time would tell.

She spent the night tossing and turning.

In the end, she had spent longer than normal at her toilette. She had tried to be inconspicuous about her plans as she asked her maid to pin up her hair, being more particular than usual.

She wished she could leave off her black, but she would just have to make do. Giving her cheeks a pinch to add some colour to her face, she gave herself a once-over and with a shrug, grabbed her shawl, a warm cloak, and headed out towards the pavilion.

Sarah arrived early, so it did not surprise her to find herself alone.

It was a sunny day; the sunlight trickling through the canopy overhead lit the pavilion beautifully. Despite the dead foliage, there was something fantastical about this place. Sarah wondered why they had fallen out of fashion. Her wistful contemplation was interrupted by the sound of someone clearing their throat.

She turned and saw to both her relief and embarrassment that William Thorne had appeared in the clearing.

"Mr. Thorne," she said with a small curtsey.

"Good morning, Lady Askew," he said, doffing his hat.

Now that he was in front of her, she did not know what to say. Her gloved hands twitched for something to do. She suddenly felt awkward and unsure of herself.

"I received your letter. I do apologize again for startling you yesterday." He spoke in that loud, clear voice of his.

It seemed to echo about the pavilion. The next time he spoke it was softer as though fearing the echo would draw the attention of others.

"I was just surprised when you opened the door. It

didn't help that I was not ready to have this conversation yet," Sarah said. She walked around to the other side of the structure as though trying to put more space between them. "I also had an ulterior motive," she said with a smile. "I promised Mr. Featherston I would do my best to convince you to restore this pavilion. It holds special memories for him, and to be honest, I find it quite spectacular even now with winter approaching."

His face fell at her words. "You have grown quite close to him."

"Yes, I have, but I am asking this favour so that he might return the favour by setting matters straight with his mother," she said.

"What do you mean?" he said, walking closer to one of the pillars, a hand touching the stone, something similar to what she had done when she had first seen the pavilion.

"He will ensure his parents know that we are not engaged nor have any plans of being so," she said, noticing the change in his countenance immediately. She hid a smile.

"Ah."

Emboldened, she walked around until she was standing in front of him bold as a tom cat.

"Mr. Thorne, what you wrote in your letter surprised me. You were always warning me away from fortune-hunting suitors, and yet I seem to have come across one just the same," she said. "Were you saving me for yourself?"

He looked amused by her boldness.

"And if I was?"

She merely shrugged. "I don't know."

"Do you feel nothing for me then? I would not pressure you into any sort of relationship that you did not want. I would never speak of my feelings towards you again. We would be as we were."

"At each other's throats?" she asked, hesitating slightly at the innuendo, but she remained firm.

"I suppose we weren't always on the friendliest of terms," he said, his smile disappearing.

"I found you quite infuriating at times, but...truth be told, I also enjoyed the time we spent together. I never hoped for anything close to love. I was content with the status quo, and I could have been happy to merely be respected by my partner in life. But as of late I started thinking...what if there was more to life? That's when I became determined to remain on my own for the rest of my life. It didn't help that I was written out of society as having some curse hanging over my head." She took a breath, walking away from him to find the pillar with the poem. His eyes followed her. "Then something changed and...perhaps it was you. I came to dream of something more, and then out of nowhere your letter arrived. Why would anyone care for me in that way? I realized how much I had come to admire you."

She stopped, realizing how much she was rambling. She walked back towards him but found herself retreating again from his approaching form. She couldn't unsay what she had just said. Her back was up against the stone pillar. She could feel the jagged stone digging into her back.

He loomed over her, his face hidden in shadow. Her knees threatened to buckle from underneath her; she was so mortified by what she had said, and he was so close now. She couldn't bear it.

"What did you say?" His voice was a whisper.

"That...I...admire you," she said, her head down, happy for the privacy her hat afforded her.

A finger tilted her chin up. Her head was spinning, ready for him to laugh at her or say something to cut her heart into ribbons.

In the span of a heartbeat, there was silence. Before his lips, soft and gentle, pressed upon her own. She tilted her head up, meeting his soft and gentle kiss with her own. A groan escaped him as she returned the kiss and wrapped her arms around his neck, pulling him closer. She supposed her bravery was a result of the relief he had not rejected her.

As though sensing that moment of distraction, he broke the kiss, pulling away. Even as the world came crashing down around them, she found herself missing his warmth.

Her first instinct was to apologize or maybe to run away, or shockingly enough to pull him back towards her. She took a few deep breaths, calming herself, trying to get on steadier ground.

"You must forgive me, Sarah," he said. "I have compromised you."

Her heart skipped a beat at hearing her name escape

his lips. She took a step towards him, though he had turned away from her.

"Then you should have thought of that before you kissed me," she said, her eyebrow arching defiantly as he turned to look at her. "Did you feel no emotion when you did that? If so, then it is true you have compromised me and left me feeling like a fool, but if not..."

His fingers ran through his hair. He looked like he was battling with his inner thoughts. He reached out for her, but she resisted.

For once she was calm. Nothing but a peaceful emptiness inside. The calm before the storm. He was what she wanted. This was a desire she had expressed and had seen returned. She tilted her head.

"I expect nothing from you," she said at last. "I meant what I said. I admire you. I find myself thinking of you, enjoying your company. This is what I thought you felt too—am I wrong? But I don't claim to hold any power or influence over you. I don't expect you to marry me just because you have kissed me. If you don't want that, then tell me now. If you want something else of me, tell me... Or perhaps you have concluded that I am repugnant. But tell me now so that I should forget everything between us." She heard how wanton that sounded, but her own emotions were getting the better of her and caution was thrown to the wind.

"You don't know what you are saying," he said. "No woman would want that."

"No woman with any sense," she said, flinging his words back at him. "I have nothing to lose but my reputation, which wasn't very great to begin with. I have my settlement, and if I have to, I can live on it quietly until old age claims me. For once I want to make my own decisions. I want you, if you will have me. Are you disgusted with me for speaking so bluntly?"

She watched his every move carefully, but he remained unreadable until something seemed to crack away at his cold demeanour.

"No."

Sarah had to hide her smile; it was lucky he had spoken then because she could feel her bravery leaving her with every breath she took.

They were at a standstill. Neither seemed certain about what to do next.

"Are we to pretend nothing happened?"

"What do you suggest? I am having trouble deciding if I should call for a priest immediately or not wait a moment longer," he threw back at her, though not unkindly.

"Ca—" She was cut off by the sound of voices approaching.

Immediately they pretended as though nothing had happened.

It was Eloise and her maid walking hand in hand. Sarah's eyes moved to Eloise's large belly; it cleared Sarah's head of any desire she might have felt. There were very real consequences to what she had been about to propose. It wasn't just her reputation on the line.

Upon seeing them, Eloise waved.

"I heard about this pavilion. I wished to see it for

myself," she said, approaching. "It's a bit dreary isn't it? Perhaps you will be able to think of something for my uncle to do with it."

Sarah assured her she would try to think of something creative.

They spent a few more minutes examining the pavilion. Eloise seemed completely ignorant that she had stumbled across a clandestine meeting. Sarah found it hard to concentrate; her mind kept drifting back to the kiss. Never had a man kissed her like that before, letting her feel all the desire and want in one motion and yet the tenderness and care there as well.

"We should head back to the house; you look cold," Eloise said, noticing how red her face was. Sarah was glad for the biting wind.

"A very good idea," Sarah said, stealing a glance at Mr. Thorne. He seemed distracted by the pavilion, studying it intently.

"Shall we head back, William?" Eloise said.

Sarah's eyes met his.

"If Lady Askew will stay for tea," he said, perfectly eloquent.

It irked Sarah that he could appear so calm at a time like this.

They walked back to the house in silence, listening to Eloise recount what her husband had said in his latest letter. He would be discharged by the New Year and he had a few places to see before he would come to whisk Eloise home.

"I shall miss Oakham a lot. Perhaps I can persuade

him to let me stay here. What do you think, William?" she asked.

"Whatever you wish, but I think when the time comes you will be more comfortable under your own roof."

"Fair, and who knows what improvements you will be in the middle of making," Eloise said.

They were served tea in the drawing room. Sarah was abnormally quiet, and this did not go unnoticed by Eloise.

"Is something the matter?"

Sarah shook her head. "I suppose I am distracted, thinking of my own trip back home."

This seemed to surprise Mr. Thorne, even though he had known of it for some time and had even hired her a private carriage to escort her.

"Is it time already?" Eloise said. "I cannot believe how fast time is passing us by."

"I wouldn't be surprised if it snowed any day now," Sarah said.

"It hardly snows this far south," Mr. Thorne chimed in, their eyes locking again. "The weather is very fair."

Sarah had to look away.

"I should return home," she said, standing. "Thank you for your hospitality." She bowed to them both and left after they each said goodbye.

She was out the door when Mr. Thorne's voice called after her.

"Shall I escort you, Lady Askew?"

"You had better not, Mr. Thorne. I think we both

have a lot of thinking to do," she said, managing a small smile. "I am flattered by the attention you've been paying me."

"You should not be so surprised," he said but seemed to understand that she was asking for space. "I shall see you soon. I hope. Good day, Lady Askew."

"Good day," she said, thinking that she preferred hearing the way he said her first name.

The next few days were busy, keeping up with work sent her way by Mrs. Greencroft and Mrs. Reed. They had called to celebrate her little victory, letting her know that they had each received a visit from Mrs. Rodes.

"You would be proud of how well we played our parts. I think I'll take part in the next Christmas pageant," Mrs. Reed said, a wide grin on her face.

"I am grateful you didn't give away our little game," Sarah said, then a pang of guilt hit her. "I do feel as though it was wrong to have tricked her like this. I do not like lying."

"You were lying for a greater purpose. Besides, you didn't technically lie. You omitted certain truths," Mrs. Greencroft said. "By the way, I am glad to see you out of those clothes. You look reborn."

Sarah looked down at her feet to hide a blush. "Thank you, I feel spoiled for choice now."

She had chosen a forest-green gown and had pinned a sprig of holly in her cap in honour of the upcoming festive season. Out of respect, since she was in half-mourning, she still wore a black armband.

"When are you setting out for your journey? You must be missing your parents terribly."

"This coming Monday. I hope the roads will be good."

They did not stay long as the wind outside seemed to be picking up; fearing a storm, the ladies piled into Mrs. Greencroft's waiting carriage.

Sarah had been impressed with herself; she had managed to go several days without seeing Mr. Thorne, though she had visited Eloise often. She had seemed to flourish now that Miss Glousen wasn't there to influence her. Eloise herself had confided how Miss Glousen had constantly been egging her on to make extravagant purchases, and had led her to believe she would be seen as inferior to others unless she did everything right. Which usually entailed sending for the latest fashions or throwing over-the-top parties. Approaching motherhood had mellowed out her unsettled nature. She was more likely to be pleased simply doing some needlework, or reading a good book, and was more interested in the day-to-day running of the estate.

The day of her departure, Sarah had seen to her packed trunks and left instructions to her housekeeper. Her maid was already in the carriage, which was filled not only with her things but warm wool blankets and furs for the journey.

She headed to say farewell to Eloise and Mr. Thorne,

unable to keep herself from feeling a thrill of excitement at the prospect of seeing him again.

She was so lost in her thoughts that she had not seen him waiting along the path.

"Lady Askew," he said with some amusement.

She nearly jumped out of her skin. "Pardon me, I did not see you there, Mr. Thorne."

"I feared I would not be able to speak to you alone..."

His words made her heart pound in her chest.

"Oh."

He smiled. "Have you had much time to think?"

"Quite a long time," she said, finding it hard to meet his eyes as her gaze kept travelling down to his lips.

"I have a proposition for you, if you are keen to hear me out."

The way he said it was so business-like that she blinked a few times.

"By all means," Sarah said.

"I think it would be in our best interests for us to be done with all this dancing between us. It would be shameful to keep skirting about the issue," he began, and she felt constricted, as though a hand was squeezing her heart. "It would be worse for our reputation for any more dilly-dallying to occur."

"I understand," she interrupted him, unable to hear the rejection or let him continue in this manner.

"Do you?" he said, his eyebrow arching. "No, I don't think you do," he continued, tilting her face up so she was forced to look at him. She could feel the tell-tale sign of tears pricking her eyes. "For I mean to marry you, if you will have me, Sarah."

She nearly fainted, but she was glad she didn't. Tears were streaming down her face now, but out of relief. "I will, William."

His smile seemed to illuminate his face.

"Then I feel safe to do this..." He wrapped his arms around her, pulling her close to him before kissing her again. This time the kiss was firmer, more insistent, and Sarah met his passion with her own.

They broke apart at last, laughing.

"What will we tell everyone?" she said.

"That you worked some magic upon a heartless beast," he suggested.

She rolled her eyes, accepting the arm he offered as they walked. "I think we should keep this a secret between us until I am out of mourning. Otherwise, I am sure the newspapers and gossip-mongers would have a field day. I will tell my parents over Christmas. They might forbid my coming back until things are settled between us, as it wouldn't be proper."

He frowned. "Maybe you don't tell them and come back safe and sound."

"Are you suggesting I keep a secret?" she said in mock indignation. Her exuberant mood was catching, and he joined her in jest.

"I might even recommend a hasty elopement. The carriage is already packed and waiting," he teased.

Sarah blushed. "I-I don't think I am ready for that."

"Very well. Then we face a long estrangement."

She stole a sidelong glance at him and with a grin said, "I have heard that absence makes the heart grow fonder."

She gasped as she found herself suddenly twirled around and assaulted with a trail of kisses, from the base of her neck to her ready lips.

"Mr. Thorne, someone might see," she reprimanded him when at last he stopped.

"In what other way do you recommend I reprimand you for such cheek?" he said with a Cheshire cat grin.

"I could think of a few..."

Printed in Great Britain
by Amazon